"What if we find a hidden message in that photo? Who do *we* report it to? How can we know it's not the wrong person?"

Hillary mulled it over for all of ten seconds. "I go to *my* chain of command."

He nodded grimly. "Okay. If we find something useful, you take it up your chain of command. Then duck, because if this extends across the Alliance, we're going to take a dangerous ride."

"I think neither of us has ever avoided danger."

He then said something he figured she wouldn't like because she was so strong. But it burst from his heart anyway. "I couldn't stand it if anything happened to you."

She didn't bristle, not even a bit. Her answer was simple. "Nor I to you." Then she returned to Valkyrie Hillary. "We have a mission."

CONARD COUNTY: TRACES OF MURDER

New York Times Bestselling Author

RACHEL LEE

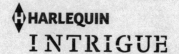

To my daughter who deserves angel's wings.

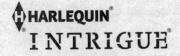

HARLEQUIN®
INTRIGUE®

ISBN-13: 978-1-335-40178-6

Conard County: Traces of Murder

Copyright © 2021 by Susan Civil-Brown

Recycling programs
for this product may
not exist in your area.

Harlequin Enterprises ULC
22 Adelaide St. West, 40th Floor
Toronto, Ontario M5H 4E3, Canada
www.Harlequin.com

Printed in U.S.A.

Rachel Lee was hooked on writing by the age of twelve and practiced her craft as she moved from place to place all over the United States. This *New York Times* bestselling author now resides in Florida and has the joy of writing full-time.

Books by Rachel Lee

Harlequin Intrigue

Conard County: The Next Generation

Cornered in Conard County
Missing in Conard County
Murdered in Conard County
Conard County Justice
Conard County: Hard Proof
Conard County: Traces of Murder

Harlequin Romantic Suspense

Conard County: The Next Generation

Snowstorm Confessions
Undercover Hunter
Playing with Fire
Conard County Witness
A Secret in Conard County
A Conard County Spy
Conard County Marine
Undercover in Conard County
Conard County Revenge
Conard County Watch
Stalked in Conard County

Visit the Author Profile page at Harlequin.com.

CAST OF CHARACTERS

Hillary Kristiansen—A member of an elite Norwegian all-female special operations unit, she helps Trace with his investigation.

Trace Mullen—A member of 101st Airborne, US Army, he seeks his best friend's murderer.

Stan Witherspoon—He's a murderer and an employee of a weapons manufacturer.

Maude—She's the cranky owner of the City Café.

Gage Dalton—He's longtime sheriff of Conard County.

Chapter One

On a gray day, Hillary Kristiansen stood on a wind-swept hill in Conard County, Wyoming. She faced a gravestone, holding yellow roses in her hand.

Brigid L. Mannerly, United States Army
Bravely served
Bravely died for her country.

"Brigid," she murmured, grief welling up in her. She hadn't known Brigid for all that long, but from the moment Hillary had met her, they had bonded like sisters. Brigid's death had carved a deep, dark hole in Hillary's heart.

It seemed like a lifetime ago that they'd made promises to visit one another at home when they both got leave at the same time. Now this was the only way Hillary could keep her promise. Standing beside a cold grave.

Blinking back salty tears, Hillary squatted and laid the roses on Brigid's grave. A small token of a friendship that should have spanned decades.

The chilly autumn wind bit her cheeks, a harbinger of the coming winter, but Hillary scarcely noticed. She was accustomed to a far frostier climate.

Closing her eyes, she thought of Norwegian mountains, covered with snow, tipped with glaciers. Thought of how she had promised that she would take Brigid cross-country skiing, teasing her about how slowly she would move at first, how she wouldn't be able to keep up. How Brigid had gamely replied that she'd give Hillary a run for her money. They'd both known that wouldn't be possible, but it had stolen none of the fun from their teasing.

So many possibilities buried beneath a blanket of dirt sodded over with brown grass. It wasn't the first time Hillary had suffered such a loss, but this one was somehow worse. Her friend, her sister.

A small American flag tipped near the gravestone, and Hillary reached out to straighten it and plant it more firmly. Brigid had earned every bit of that respect.

KIA. Killed in action. Every soldier knew it was possible, but few thought about it until those left behind faced the reality of each new empty place in a unit. Gone. Never to return. Then necessity required them to shrug it off. To believe they were somehow immune.

Until the nightmares began.

Gradually Hillary became aware of someone standing at the next gravesite. She wanted to ignore the stranger, didn't want his intrusion into her private grief.

Then he spoke. "You knew Brigid?"

That brought her to her feet, and she pivoted to see a tall man, his build bespeaking steel, his face bearing the scar of a single knife slash. Recognition awoke deep within. He was a soldier, too.

"Yes," she answered. "Afghanistan." She looked at Brigid's grave again. Some rose petals had loosened and wafted away on the wind. Apropos. *Fly away, Brigid.*

She spoke again. "Do you know her husband? I was thinking about calling, if he wouldn't mind."

A pause. Then a gut punch in the form of taut words. "Allan is dead, too."

He pointed to the gravestone next to Brigid's. "Two months ago. They say it was suicide."

Hillary's heart clenched as she absorbed the shock, as she sensed that this man didn't believe it was suicide at all.

"Herregud," she whispered. "Good God."

His face hardened. "I came here to visit them both. We were friends since childhood."

She met his gaze, seeing eyes as gray as the sky overhead. "That is a shame."

He gave a sharp nod. "Definitely." Then he paused. "You sound British."

"My mother."

He looked down at the stones again. "Let me buy you a coffee. We're going to freeze out here."

She doubted she'd freeze, but the invitation was welcome. They could talk about Brigid, about Allan. About all that had happened. She needed that, and she suspected he did, too.

He held out his hand. "Apologies. I'm Trace Mullen."

"Hillary Kristiansen," she answered as she returned his shake.

They walked side by side to the parking lot, she in her dark wool slack suit and a light jacket, he in jeans with an open peacoat. His bare head displayed short dark hair, almost black. Around here, she thought, her own tightly cropped, pale blond hair probably stood out, flying in the face of her training. She wished for a watch cap.

In her rental, Hillary followed him into town, a small, quaint place she liked instantly. Brigid had spoken warmly of Conard City, of Conard County. Her heart had been here, and not just because of Allan.

Trace led the way to a small diner labeled the City Café. Inside, the booths and tables announced their age, red vinyl seats repaired in places with matching tape. A few older men had ensconced themselves in a far corner, having drawn tables together.

The two of them chose a table as far away as they could get. Some semblance of privacy.

A heavyset woman with a grumpy attitude took their coffee orders. "You'll be wanting some pie or cobbler," she said before stalking away.

Trace spoke. "That's Maude. She's a fixture, and I don't think I've ever seen her smile."

"If the coffee is good…" Hillary tried to summon a smile.

"Oh, it is. So is everything she cooks and bakes here. She's still giving Melinda's bakery a run for her money."

Casual conversation about nothing, a slow feeling out of one another.

"So," Trace said after the coffee arrived with a thud, "you're half British? You're in the British Army?"

"No. My father is Norwegian. I am Jegertroppen." The all-female unit of Special Operations.

He stared at her, raising his brows. "The Hunters. The Valkyries."

"So we are called."

"Good God. The BBC called you the toughest women in the world."

She didn't know how to answer that, especially since she wasn't feeling all that tough right then. She switched tack. "And you? Army?" It seemed a likely conclusion, given that Brigid and her husband had both been in the Army.

"One hundred and first Airborne."

She wasn't surprised. She'd sensed something about him at the cemetery, something more than *soldier*. And Brigid had mentioned her husband's unit. She spoke, using a phrase she had heard applied to the Airborne. "Death from the skies."

At that he smiled faintly. "I never had the pleasure of working with anyone from Jegertroppen."

"Just as well. I doubt it would have been an enjoyable situation." She waved generally toward the window. "Brigid talked about the mountains here."

"Probably not what you're used to."

"Depends on where you are. We have some flatlands, too. However, we did have a reason to invent the cambered ski. Long winters and a need to get around in those mountains." Surprising them both, pieces of fruit pie landed in front of them. Before they could express their gratitude, Maude had stormed off.

Trace spoke. "I guess we were offending her natural order of things."

They were also avoiding their primary concern. Hillary wondered how to divert them back to it but couldn't see a polite way. She decided to eat some berry pie and wait. Not that she felt very hungry. Her usual strenuous life had given her a healthy appetite, but grief changed everything. She pecked at the pie.

Trace didn't seem much more interested. "I heard you train with the US Navy SEALs?"

"Sometimes." Hillary shrugged it off. "For certain kinds of operations. I don't want to talk about me. Right now I'd prefer to leave that part behind. I'm here for Brigid."

"I know." He frowned slightly. "You'd better eat at least half that pie, or Maude will be insulted. Life with an insulted Maude could become complicated when you're hungry."

Then he turned his attention back. "Brigid. And Allan. Like I said, I knew them all my life. We grew up here. I won't say we never had our disagreements or that we occasionally didn't have different groups of friends. Youngsters are like that."

He looked straight at her. "But there was no one in this town less surprised than I when they decided to get married. There was an unbreakable bond between them despite the inevitable ups and downs. It always felt like destiny."

Hillary nodded, forcing herself to eat another forkful of pie, mindful of not upsetting the locals. "Did you all enlist at the same time?"

He gave a crooked smile. "Never hesitated. We talked about it for years, then did it. The Army was the first thing that separated us."

"It has a way of doing that. Physically, at any rate."

"It does. We had different paths to follow for a while. But the closeness remained. What about you and Brigid?"

"We met at an operating base. It was instant friendship." She paused. "Brigid talked a lot about Allan. She missed him every minute of every day."

"He felt the same. If they regretted anything about their choices, that was it."

Hillary put her fork down, refusing to force any more pie down her throat.

"I miss her," she said quietly. "So much." The Norwegian words came first to her tongue. *"Det er som om hjertet mitt har blitt revet ut."* Then remembering him, she translated, "I feel as if my heart has been torn out."

"Pretty much the same here."

He'd lost *two* friends, she reminded herself. Did that double the grief or just make it a hell of a lot worse? Could grief even be measured?

His somber expression matched her mood. So much pain between the two of them. Maybe she should just end this visit now. She had no comfort to offer. She doubted he did, either.

Off to their separate worlds to deal with the gaping abyss in their lives.

When he spoke again, it was another diversion. "Was it hard to make it into the Valkyries?"

"It is never easy."

"Like the women being admitted to the Rangers. No slack."

"Slack would make us useless." Undeniable. Special operations allowed no weakness. "Brigid was talking about training into spec ops."

"Allan mentioned it. She wasn't entirely happy with guarding convoys."

"Dangerous enough. Obviously." Too obviously. "Allan?"

"He wasn't exactly thrilled with the idea, but he never would have interfered." Trace paused a few beats. "Did Brigid tell you? Allan was invalided out, discharged for medical reasons. Too much shrapnel in dangerous places, and they couldn't remove it. Near his heart. Threatening his spine. He hated it."

"I can imagine."

"But he felt the greatest pride in Brigid. He wouldn't have dishonored her."

Then Trace leaned forward and lowered his voice. "Someone killed him."

Chapter Two

The words tasted like ashes as they left Trace's mouth. He could see the shock ripple through Hillary and waited for her to argue with him. To turn away and go back to her life. How could she possibly believe him? How could he possibly explain?

Outwardly, she remained impassive. "Why do they think he committed suicide?"

"Post-traumatic stress compounded by grief."

She nodded. "Makes sense."

"Of course it makes sense. It fits right in with the easy explanation. The too-obvious one."

"Okay. But why don't you believe it?"

"Because he wasn't one to give up. Because he told me he'd get through it. Because he and Brigid had promised each other not to do it. I've known Allan my entire life. He never broke a promise."

She looked away, staring out the window, absorbing, evaluating. As difficult as it had been to speak the words out loud, it must be equally difficult for her to accept them. Plus, she hadn't known Allan. How could she judge?

She sighed after a bit and returned her gaze to him.

The pale blue eyes so often found in Nordic people. The pale, pale blond hair. High cheekbones, an athletic body trimmed by constant training. A very attractive woman.

He brushed the thought aside. Not the time. He had more important matters on his mind. Allan. His friend for over thirty years. A man who had never bent to anything. Who'd never been broken. Not even his wife's death could have made him give up the fight. *I'll get through this.* The words were stamped in Trace's mind. He'd never doubted them, even though Allan had begun to drink heavily.

Hillary drew a deep breath, searching his face. "You're saying he was murdered."

The ugly word hung on the air, a word he'd never allowed himself to say. *Killed*, yes. But murdered? No. Though it was the same thing.

"Do you have any ideas?" Hillary asked. "Enemies he might have had?"

"None that I'm aware of."

She shook her head slightly. "Then who? Why?"

"I'm going to figure that out. I swear. I owe it to him. To Brigid. This is a stain on my friend's memory, and if there's any way I can prove it, I will."

She appeared to understand that. Now she nodded slightly.

"Let's get out of here," he said abruptly. "I don't know about you, but I can't sit still for too long. My body requires activity."

SHE FULLY UNDERSTOOD THAT. Muscles so finely honed needed to move. Sitting on a plane for a long flight could be a form of torture, causing her to twitch, tightening every muscle until it could relax again. People who sat next to her must often be annoyed.

He tossed money on the table and led the way outside. Standing in the endless wind, concentrated by the narrow street, she once again felt the bite of cold.

"Are you going to stay in town for a while?"

"I had thought a few days."

"You gonna be warm enough?" he asked. "I'm thinking about taking a long walk, maybe do some running, if you'd like to."

She'd have liked to say she was fine but faced reality. There was nothing to be gained by toughing this out, even for a few days. "Yes, a jacket would be nice. I didn't bring one." Because she hadn't expected to be here long enough to care. Because she was on her way to warmer climates.

"Let's go to the Mercantile. We'll find something you like well enough."

She looked down at her feet, glad she'd at least worn her boots. Pretty shoes didn't usually fit in her wardrobe, although she had a pair of sandals in her suitcase back at the airport for her impending trip to the South of France. No good here.

He led her around a corner and down a street to a large, old building. Surprisingly few people were about on the streets, but to everyone they met Trace gave a nod.

The Mercantile held the musty smell of an old building. Wooden floors creaked beneath their feet. Trace led her to a section of women's clothing. Part of her resented that, because she often bought men's clothing, and part of her recognized that she needed something to fit her smaller frame. None of the frilly stuff, though, and she hated pink.

Her first choice was the watch cap she'd thought of earlier. Then she found a white and navy down vest that fit well enough, followed by a dark blue windproof winter jacket. Layers.

Insulated gloves as well. She paid with a credit card, asked the clerk to remove all the tags then pulled on her new acquisitions. "Ready."

He nodded. They strode out of the store with purpose, nearly a march, and took a turn toward the nearer mountains. Their pace was brisk, determined. This was necessary exercise, not a casual stroll.

Unconsciously they fell in step, their strides matching perfectly. Training. Practice. Custom.

As the ground began to rise a mile or so beyond town, Hillary felt ready to run. Rising land beneath her feet was always a cue. But her run wasn't all-out. It was measured for maximum endurance. Long runs couldn't be taken at top speed.

She felt light as a feather without her full complement of combat gear. This was easy, maybe too easy. Trace trotted alongside her. Before long, their breathing became as synchronized as their footfalls.

The slope continued to steepen, but not so much it was a serious challenge. The road became dirt, easier on the knees than pavement, but harder on the ankles because it was uneven. Pine scents filled the air. A few late wildflowers dotted the roadside.

When at last they reached the top of a rise, Trace called a halt. "Stretched out?" he asked.

"For now." Turning, she looked back down toward the valley and saw the town, resembling a model that could have fit in a display case. Then she looked at Trace. He was no more out of breath than she.

"How," she asked, "do you intend to find this killer?"

"I haven't the foggiest idea. Allan and Brigid left me their house. I haven't wanted to go in there yet, but it's crossed my mind I might find a clue. A direction. Or maybe the grapevine will whisper in my ear."

He sighed heavily and paced, bending occasionally to stretch. Hillary followed suit. Her jacket was plenty warm, as was her vest beneath it, and the run had heated her legs.

His plan was amorphous. Clutching at straws. Not that she blamed him, not when he thought Allan had been murdered.

No one could leave that alone.

But it didn't seem like there was any good starting point. A quixotic quest?

He spoke again. "How did your parents meet?"

The question surprised her, coming out of the blue. Another diversion from the impossible?

"My mother's father was the British ambassador to Norway. They met at an official function and married rather quickly. I was born quickly, too."

He stared out over the valley. "This doesn't sound like a happy ending."

"It wasn't," she admitted. "They separated when I was eight. Mother went back to England, and I chose to stay with my father. Of course, I visited my mother every summer and some holidays, but I was Norwegian in my own mind. In my heart."

"Not a bad thing to be. What does your father do?"

"Army special operations," she answered simply.

"So it runs in the family?"

"It does now."

That brought a smile to his face, and she was glad to see it. Grieving didn't preclude moments of amusement or even happiness. Not that she was feeling either right then.

"What are you going to do?" she asked again.

"Damned if I know. When we get back, let's go to their house. I can't think of anywhere else to start looking for clues. Especially since the whole damned town believes Allan offed himself."

She was agreeable, if only to help him over the emotional bump he was likely to face when he entered that house. He'd already said he was avoiding it. Memories must swarm there, ready to sting him like wasps.

Jogging uphill hadn't been difficult, but running back down was easier and brought them both to a quickened pace. The sound of their thudding feet, perfectly in time, felt so familiar to Hillary that tension unwound in her and deep relaxation followed. When they reached the town again, Trace suggested dropping by Maude's, as he called the City Café, to recover their parked cars and pick up some food.

"We're going to need it after that run. Any preferences?"

"Fish, but I didn't see that on the menu. You choose."

The town was a bit busier now, and Hillary noticed the stares she received. She tried to return them all with a smile but figured by nightfall everyone was going to be wondering who she was.

Well, let them wonder. She just didn't want them to know the extent of her military background. That would probably raise a whole lot of questions. Not that she cared about the questions. She'd be gone tomorrow or the next day, and they could all enjoy speculating.

Except that her desire to go back to her original plans was fading in the face of Trace's concerns. What if Allan *hadn't* died by suicide? What if there was still something she needed to do for Brigid?

The question hung over her now, darker than the sky overhead.

MAUDE RAISED AN eyebrow over the size of Trace's order, but she was probably wondering if he meant to eat it all himself. He didn't bother explaining that two people who had just finished fifteen road miles needed to fuel up.

Jegertroppen, huh? A truly elite group. Trace hadn't let himself really think about that before, but he was impressed. He knew the kind of training he'd undergone to become Airborne, and he suspected hers had been as extreme. Up and down those Norwegian mountains in full battle kit, running or skiing. And that was just the beginning. They might well have taught the SEALs a thing or two.

Hillary waited in her rental outside, and he supposed her eyebrows were raising like Maude's as he stepped out with four plastic bags filled to the brim and a tray of four hot coffees.

He manhandled them into his vehicle and drove slowly with her right behind him. Allan and Brigid had had a tidy little house at the western end of town, where most of the houses began to spread away from each other, leaving a nice-size lawn. Looking at it, he decided he really needed to get out the lawn mower. Thus far he'd paid a couple of guys to do the job, but it appeared they hadn't been here in a few weeks. Not that there was much left to do. The grasses were turning brown and yellow in the face of the approaching winter. Still, a few green blades poked up bravely, reaching for sunlight that was getting too thin and watery.

Or maybe he'd just let it go. Before long even the bravest greenery would give up the fight.

Hillary was quick to help him carry the bags as he approached the front door with the tray of coffees. His steps grew heavier as he drew closer. The last time he'd entered, Allan had been there. That damn house was going to feel so very empty.

Not only were his steps heavier, but so was his heart. The ache in his chest grew tighter, like a band that wanted to suffocate him. This wasn't his first loss, but this one was closer. Much closer.

He fumbled the key from his pocket and pushed it into the lock. A bit rusty, it resisted slightly but then turned. He pushed open the door.

The house smelled stale now. Even the cleaning fluids from the people he'd hired to remove the stains of Allan's death had evaporated into nothing. Empty. Every sense in his body noticed.

Hillary followed him, her watch cap shoved into a pocket. Her steps sounded gentler, as if she felt she trod upon holy ground. He turned. "Let's put these bags in the kitchen."

She followed him. The counters had gathered some dust, but not enough that he felt inclined to wipe it away. Everything was familiar. Too familiar. He didn't think he could bear to go into the living room, where he, Allan and Brigid had spent so many hours. The kitchen was bad enough.

Beers at that table. Brigid or Allan sometimes pulling something sweet and tasty out of the fridge. But mostly it had been pretzels and nuts. Their own private little bar.

He sighed, heard the break in his breath. He'd seen and felt plenty of sorrow over the years, but Allan was different.

"We can go somewhere else," Hillary said.

He shook his head. "Time to face up to it all."

They ate out of foam containers because Trace didn't want to see the familiar dishes. A bit at a time, he told himself. Just one step at a time.

When Hillary sat across from him at the table, the air seemed to clear a bit. As if her mere presence were changing a mood, an aura. Relief eased the iron band around his chest.

She asked, "This is your house now?"

"Yes. I don't know that I'd ever want to live here, though."

She reached for an onion ring. "I'm not sure I would, either."

Food, he reminded himself. Eat. That run had felt good, but it required fuel. He'd eaten in the worst conditions. He could manage it now.

Food helped, bringing him back from the precipice. As his stomach filled and his cells responded, his mind responded, too, lifting his mood somewhat. He realized that Hillary's presence was not only changing the aura in here, but it was recreating his mental image of this room. Earlier memories gave way a bit to this new one.

He watched her look around the kitchen, as if she were trying to imagine Brigid in the room. He wondered if he should tell her that none of the three of them had been into cooking. When they gathered, it was almost always with takeout. Subs or frozen pizza from the grocery, baked goods from Melinda's, big meals from Maude's. Time spent down at Mahoney's Bar, eating fried chicken over tall, icy glasses of draft beer.

"Ah, hell," he said quietly.

Hillary looked up from the onion rings she was working on. "Memories?"

"Of course. Good ones, but now they'll be only memories."

She shoved food his way. "As you said, we need food after that run. And there'll be another run before this day is over. Eat up, soldier."

That dragged a smile from him. "Feeling antsy?"

"Antsy?" She frowned at the word.

"As in restless. Fidgety."

She nodded. "All that training. I'm not exhausted yet."

"We'll work on that." But he also knew that while she might feel antsy right then, her training had taught her to remain as still as an ice statue when necessary. A different kind of tension.

He reached for half a club sandwich. Time to answer necessity.

OUTSIDE, STAN WITHERSPOON stood wondering. Who was that woman Trace Mullen had taken into the house with him?

Hanging around Conard City for the last couple of months had given him a familiarity with the local people. That woman wasn't local. He'd never have missed that tousled blond hair. There wasn't much of it since it was cut so short, but that color was remarkable.

And here he'd begun to think that he would be safe if he left this county.

He watched her carry the four big bags while Mullen carried a tray of coffees. He watched the man fish in his pocket for keys, watched him open the door, watched the woman follow.

And now they were inside, beyond his ability to see what they were doing.

Uneasiness stalked him, but that was nothing new. He'd stayed here, using up a sizable chunk of his stateside rotation from his job working for a major contractor in the Middle East, because he'd been told to. The work with the contractor was tough, so the company insisted that every employee spend six months at home every few years. They didn't want any of them to "go native."

Crap. He hadn't gone native. He'd merely found a

way to make money on the situation. And that money stream had been threatened. Worse, his own life was in danger because his boss in this operation would kill him if the truth got out.

He'd come to this godforsaken place explicitly to kill Allan Mannerly. For cover he used the community college as his reason for being here.

He'd been afraid of leaving before matters calmed down after Allan Mannerly's death. It hadn't taken long for the authorities to declare the death to be suicide.

Stan should have been happy with that. After all, he'd done a good enough job to mislead the authorities. As long as nothing else was suspected, Stan was in the clear. Right?

He'd decided to stay in this place because he didn't want to bug out too soon. Didn't want to draw any kind of attention, even after the verdict. Careful. He had to be careful. As he'd so often been warned.

Or maybe that was his conscience keeping him here, not the order. Regardless, he'd begun to hear that the Mullen guy didn't believe the death to be suicide. Everyone shook their heads sadly when the subject arose, Stan among them, but they thought Mullen was being affected by his grief.

"Out of his mind," some said.

God, Stan thought, walking away from the house. God. Would he have to kill that Mullen guy, too? He didn't exactly have a taste for murder, but self-protection was a higher priority.

And who the hell was that woman?

Chapter Three

After they finished eating, Hillary helped Trace store the large quantity of leftovers. Another meal at least.

"You were too generous," she told Trace.

"I guess so, but I don't do cooking, so it's all good."

"I'm not going to volunteer to cook," she said. "I have done so little in so many years that I can't guarantee edibility." Then she added a touch of humor. "I'm also unsure if I still know how to use a pot when it's not on a campfire."

He shrugged. "Being a bachelor, I was fond of the chow hall and local restaurants when I was stateside."

She imagined that Trace, like she, had spent quite a bit of time eating with friends when they weren't training or on a mission. She had a lot of good memories from such times.

But what now? she wondered as she dried her hands on a towel. There were still two cups of coffee in foam containers, and it would be rude of her to just leave it. Making a decision, she sat down once again and reached for one of the coffees.

Trace settled across from her and took the remaining beverage.

"This is awful," Trace said eventually. "You came here to visit Brigid's grave and maybe speak to Allan. Instead you find out he's dead and you meet me, a guy who is just making you sadder."

"Stop," she said mildly. "It is what it is, I believe the saying goes. I don't regret meeting you. I'm glad you told me about Allan—well, not glad, but I think you know what I mean. I needed to know, and all I can believe is that at least he's not suffering."

"Which is better than I can say for the two of us." Again that crooked, mirthless half smile. "We make a sorry pair."

"Sorry pair," she repeated. "I may have a British mother, but I'm not familiar with all colloquialisms. My mother had a proper education in all the best schools. I suspect I may have missed quite a bit of common English."

His smile widened a shade. "I bet you know more Norwegian colloquialisms than *I* ever will. *Sorry pair* means sad pair."

"Der er ugler i mosen." She looked almost impish. "There are owls in the bog."

He raised his brows. "Meaning?"

"I believe you would say something is not quite right."

That at last drew a chuckle from him. "I'd never have guessed, but that's a good description." His face tightened. "Also quite true right now."

"You sincerely believe this about Allan." It felt uncomfortable to ask, but she needed to know this conviction wasn't momentary, born from grief.

"I do," he replied. "I absolutely do. I realize you never had a chance to know him, Hillary, but I knew him all my life. Even in the midst of this, he wouldn't have quit. Drink himself into oblivion most nights? Sure. But he would have kept going. Allan didn't have quit in him."

But Allan, perhaps, had never met a grief quite this big. On the other hand, looking at Trace, she knew *he* believed it.

"Want to go for another run?" he asked abruptly.

Part of her wanted to, but part of her had to recognize her need for rest or she'd be useless to anyone tomorrow. "Jet lag," she told him. "I flew directly from Norway. I think I need a hotel."

"You might feel a little like you're on a mission if you stay in our motel. Listen, you should stay here in the guest room. That's where Allan and Brigid would have put you. If you won't be bothered by sleeping here."

"No, it won't bother me. Are you sure?"

He rose. "Absolutely. Brigid would want it. I believe there are sheets on the bed, but I'll go check, then I'll be on my way."

A short time later, after she brought in her duffel, she watched from the window as he drove away. Was he going on another run? She wished she didn't feel as if the world was beginning to spin, because she would have liked that, too.

He'd said he'd be back in the morning, and then maybe she'd discuss the kernel of an idea that was growing within her. After some time to think it over. She did very little on impulse.

Being alone gave her an opportunity, though. Hillary could wander through rooms and imagine what this house had been like when the Mannerlys had lived here. She had no clear image of Allan, except for some photos Brigid had shared, but she had a pretty good idea.

They would have laughed a lot. Brigid was usually cheerful and ready to laugh. She couldn't imagine that Allan could have been much different, at least when he was around her.

The house itself was from more than half a century ago, she guessed. The furnishings all appeared to be secondhand, in keeping with a military income. In keeping with the fact that they wouldn't be here most of the year. A sofa, a recliner, some occasional tables. There was, however, a gaping hole in the living room, which, judging by the rug and clean wall behind, had been the place where Allan had died. Unfortunately, she had seen too much to even have to imagine it.

The chair was gone, probably a match for the one that sat at an angle. Brigid's chair, she guessed, an older plaid recliner.

The TV was relatively new, however, a big flat screen on the wall over a covered fireplace. On the mantel were a DVD player, a stereo receiver and some other pieces. Unlike everything else in this house, they appeared to be relatively new. A splurge?

Heavy insulating curtains, navy blue, covered the windows. A cozy room except for the empty spot.

The master bedroom boasted a queen-size four-poster bed covered by a cheerful comforter in a splash of colors. Brigid had picked that out, she was sure. The same navy blue curtains covered the window beside the bed. All the usual furnishings.

Then she came upon an office. Battered wood desk, two office chairs, top-of-the-line computer. Naturally, the best for video calls between the two of them. Stacks of papers, filing cabinets... This was not going to be fun to look through.

The single bathroom boasted a claw-foot tub that had probably been in the house since its first day. A showerhead at the top of a long plumbing pipe. A plastic shower curtain decorated with fish swimming in the water. Matching towels.

A guest room, as large as the master bedroom, but showing less attention to detail. A double bed without a headboard against a wall. A wooden dresser, one straight-backed wooden chair. The same navy blue curtains. A polka-dot comforter in dark blue and white. Two plump pillows.

A second guest room, hardly larger than the office, with a single bed, a small cabinet and one hardwood chair. This bed had a black throw on it.

It was a house that said very little about the people who had lived here. Perhaps because they were home so rarely? Or because they didn't have time for kitsch? Or the taste for it?

Hillary swiftly unpacked the little she thought she'd need but didn't bother to take out more. She had a flight to catch the day after tomorrow.

After a hot shower, she climbed into the bed, beneath the comforter, and stared into the dark.

The kernel of her idea was beginning to crack open, to put forth tendrils. As she was drifting into sleep, those tendrils took root.

Maybe she wouldn't leave as soon as she'd anticipated.

Chapter Four

Hillary slept deeply but awoke more in keeping with Norway time. When she pulled back the curtain, she saw that night still blanketed the land.

She shrugged and went to take a shower. She expected cold water, that Trace must have shut down nearly everything, but the water was hot and welcome. She might be used to cold showers, but she still appreciated a hot one. Such a luxury.

Afterward, wrapped in the heavy fleece robe she'd brought with her, she found her way to the kitchen and started a rich, dark pot of coffee. There were some leftovers from Maude's, but the food was heavy and Norwegians preferred to eat later in the morning.

Sitting at the kitchen table, she at last felt the emptiness of this house. Her throat tightened, but she held back tears.

She spoke aloud. "You want me to do this, Brigid. I know. I know how much you loved Allan. He won't rest until the truth is known." *You won't rest.*

The last part grabbed her. Maybe visiting a grave didn't have to be her final act for a friend.

Even so, this seemed like a hopeless cause. How did Trace expect to learn anything the police hadn't? Or maybe he thought that the police simply hadn't looked because it would be so obvious to them.

He might be right about that. *Veteran with PTSD loses wife.* That could overwhelm anyone. And it would be the apparent conclusion.

Her heart was breaking for Trace, however. He'd lost so much in such a short period of time. As bad as the loss of Brigid had been for her, for Trace it had to be so much worse. Two lifelong friends in the space of less than a year.

Night still smothered the land when a rap on the door drew her attention. She never doubted it was Trace. Who else would show up at this hour?

When she opened the door, she found him standing there with two shopping bags.

"I thought you'd be awake," he remarked. "Can I come in?"

"Of course. There's coffee."

"Sounds great." He joined her in the kitchen. "I'm assuming you don't want to eat before a run?"

He was right about that. The coffee would be enough for now. "Where are we going?"

"Pretty much the same as yesterday. I like that hill. Or the side of that mountain." He flashed a short smile. "I hope you don't think I'm out of bounds, but these bags are for you."

Startled, she looked at them then at him. "What for?"

"You need some decent running clothes. So last evening I stopped by the department store, spoke to the very nice lady who helped you yesterday and asked her to judge your sizes. I hope she was right. Go ahead and look."

She felt a little embarrassed, as if she'd had to be rescued. "You shouldn't have."

"But I did. I like to have a companion to eat up the miles with me. Anyway, it's colder than yesterday, and I'm sure running in your dress slacks isn't the most comfortable way to go."

Hillary couldn't argue, so she began pulling items out of the bag. Fleece-lined pants in gray. A fleece shirt in the same. And at the bottom a silky thermal undergarment in dark blue that would cover her from neck to foot. There were also six pairs of new thermal socks.

"Good choices," she admitted. "Thank you."

"My experience counts for something, and I figured you hadn't come prepared for this. Do you want to run this morning?"

Her muscles ached for the activity. "Absolutely." She picked up the bags and headed for the bedroom. Everything fit well. No folds in the undergarment to irritate her. At least she'd brought her own boots. Breaking in a new pair meant blisters.

When she emerged, ready to go, he said, "You might want to bring your vest and watch cap. Wind's blowing down from the mountains."

She took his advice, and ten minutes later they were out the door. The first steel gray had begun to lighten the sky, but there was no promise the clouds would vanish. A bit of sun would have been welcome, but not necessary.

They left town behind them before there was much traffic and soon reached the point where the ground began to rise.

Hillary spoke, far from breathless. "Anything steeper?"

"Oh, yeah. A little farther ahead, we'll take a turn and test that mountain."

It sounded good to her. Her muscles stretched, loosening completely, ready for more. She loved the feeling of her legs devouring the miles. Her father had remarked that she was built for this. And for more, apparently, since she'd qualified for the Jegertroppen.

When they turned, they were no longer on the dirt road. It became a treacherous track, probably carved by off-road vehicles. By people out for some fun.

It didn't faze her. She'd run over much more dangerous ground. Being something of a mountain goat was required.

Trace ran smoothly beside her as they climbed. Her breaths became measured, deeply in, then deeply out. She heard Trace begin the same rhythm. A thought occurred to her.

"Your legs are longer," she remarked. "Am I slowing you?"

"Hardly. You've trained. We all adjust our strides."

It was true, so she cast aside the concern. They continued upward. The air became colder. Gradually she felt the air beginning to thin. Not very much.

Trace spoke. "You been training much at altitude?"

"Not lately," she admitted. "Too many low-altitude missions."

"Then we turn around. No altitude sickness, please."

She thought he was being overly cautious. Gauging that they were at about twenty-five hundred meters, that wasn't enough to make most people sick. But most people weren't running, either.

Nor did she want a round of altitude sickness. If it became bad enough, she might need a hospital.

"We can go higher if you want," he offered. "This trail goes to about thirteen thousand feet."

She did a quick mental conversion. About four thousand meters. "I guess we should shorten it. At least for a day or two."

"A day or two?" He stopped running and began jogging in place. "I thought you intended to leave tomorrow."

"I'm reconsidering. I'll be ready for your four thousand meters in a couple of days. It doesn't take long for me to acclimate."

"Probably not since you do it so often." He surprised her with a smile. "This mountain doesn't go much higher than that. Maybe after a few days we can hit the peak and run down the other side."

They began their descent at a fast clip. "Does this mountain have a name?"

"Thunder Mountain. Lots of great stories about it if you want to hear them later. Such as wolves."

She dared a glance his way. "Wolves? I thought your country had exterminated them."

"We might still. There's been an effort to restore them to the wild, with all the attendant fury among ranchers. Norway?"

"We share a small number with Sweden. About four

hundred. I suspect the disagreements are the same you have here."

"Yeah. Sometimes I see them when I run high enough."

"They seem shy, mostly. When we ski through hundreds of miles, they sometimes show up in small numbers. Never aggressive."

"Mostly curious," he agreed.

Thousands of meters disappeared beneath their feet until they reached the edge of town and the Mannerly house and passed it. An occasional car rolled by, the occupants waving.

"Friendly," she said.

"Mostly. And now I *really* want that coffee. Let's go get breakfast."

First they passed a dilapidated train depot. Next a truck stop full of grumbling trucks with a diner to one side. He led them toward the diner.

"Best breakfast around."

Well, she wasn't sure about that as she scanned the menu. While her mother had introduced her to the English fry-up, she was more accustomed to not eating at all until lunch. Anyway...

The foods she was used to were not on the menu, of course. Salmon mixed with scrambled eggs would have been nice, as would thin slices of meat on dense bread. In the end she chose the scrambled eggs, toast and a side of ham.

"Still looking for fish?" Trace asked.

She shrugged. "I eat what's available."

"I'll find you some fish at the grocery today."

"You don't have to."

"I know I don't. But I will anyway."

A very nice man, she decided. Brigid had chosen her friends well.

As they ate, he asked the inevitable question. "Why are you planning to stay longer? Not that I mind."

She thought it over, trying to decide what she could say without seeming to patronize him. This was such an important issue to him that she felt as if she needed to walk carefully.

"Brigid," she said finally. "She would want me to."

"Why?" His face appeared to have stiffened.

"Because you have questions," she answered. "Serious questions. Brigid wouldn't like them to remain unanswered if it's possible to find what happened. She wouldn't want me to walk away without trying. She wouldn't want me to walk away from her friend."

He resumed eating, appearing to ruminate. At least in Trondheim, or Afghanistan, the hour was later, and her appetite hadn't yet adjusted to the new time. She made a hearty meal once she reminded herself that this wasn't *really* breakfast.

Besides, after the run they had just taken, it wouldn't be long before hunger found her. Not long at all.

TRACE TRIED TO decide how to take her decision to stay here. It was obviously well-intentioned, but to do this because of Brigid? While *she* might be certain, he was sure that Brigid wouldn't have wanted Hillary to upend her life.

"What were you planning to do when you go home?"

he asked as they finished up. He insisted on paying the bill.

"Oh, I was thinking I would go visit some friends." One corner of her mouth lifted. "It's a good time of year to look for the sun in the South of France. January would be better, but I don't know where I'll be then."

Outside, as they began to walk the short distance to the Mannerly house, he said, "You really should keep your plans. Brigid wouldn't want you to give up your holiday."

"Maybe not. Should we argue?"

He snorted. "Not without Brigid to referee."

For the first time, he saw a genuine smile light her face. It shone almost like an internal light. God, she was beautiful.

"Well, it seems we are at a stand," she replied.

Indeed they were. He gave up. For now.

When they reached the house, he suggested she go change into something less sweaty. "I'm going to the market."

"To look for fish? Then I'll come as well."

Seemed like the safest thing, he decided. He had no idea what kind of fish she would like. Or what she might need to prepare it.

He studied her quizzically. "I thought you didn't cook. I was going to look for something prepared."

"I exaggerated. I can cook, I just don't do it very often, which keeps me out of form."

As they drove across town to the grocery, he said, "If you can't find what you want here, there's another store just up the street, a chain that's trying to move in. But people tend to be loyal to Hampstead's because it's been here for nearly a century, and because it buys most foods locally."

"Then I will try to find everything I can there."

Inside, the store was busy and everyone was friendly. Trace expected the friendliness, of course, but he was surprised at how many people paused to talk. He'd begun to feel like a pariah after the ruckus he'd raised over Allan. But Hillary was an attention-getter, all right. He introduced her only as Brigid's friend. He had no idea if she wanted him to say more.

But apparently not. She spoke with a smile, shook hands, said only that she'd be staying for a while. Her slightly British accent made her more exotic, and Trace figured the whole town would hear about her by nightfall.

The conversations were limited, however. Most shoppers had their minds on tasks at hand. Funny, he thought, how many people developed blinders when shopping for groceries. Complete oblivion.

A few offered kind words about Allan but avoided the subject of his death. It was soon certain, however, that it was Hillary who had snagged their attention, not him.

How long did she plan to stay in town? Where was she from?

Casual, mildly probing questions. She *did* let it be known she was from Norway and answered a few questions about the cold. Making conversation–type questions. Not intrusive.

Hillary hovered over the fish, most of which was frozen, given how far they were from the sea. She didn't seem to have a problem with that, but she finally asked, "Salmon fillets? With the skin on?"

She had already chosen frozen cod, but this seemed important to her.

"I don't think we have any fresh salmon around here."

She laughed. "We have salmon farms in Norway, but the fish is becoming harder to find because there's such a market in other EU countries. Higher prices, too."

"I suggest we ask the butcher. He might have some ideas."

The butcher, Ralph by name, was jovial and slightly plump. He eyed Hillary with favor.

"Don't get many requests for that around here. I think I know where to get some, but it might take a day or two. And it might be frozen."

"I'm agreeable with that."

Ralph nodded and beamed. "How much?"

"Since I'm going to teach Trace to like it, too, maybe two pounds? And thin-sliced salami and other drier sausage slices?"

Ralph took out his notebook. "Now that I can find. I take it you don't like the package stuff?"

"Not if I'm going to teach this man about Norwegian breakfast."

"Gotcha. Anything else?"

"I doubt you have a dense bread. Sort of like a baguette, but much heavier."

He shook his head. "The place to go would be the

bakery if you want it soon. Melinda can probably make you some." He winked. "But I can also try my sources."

"Thank you!"

"My pleasure. Should I call Trace when I have everything?"

"Of course," Trace answered. "Anything else?"

"I need to take a look at the cheeses. I imagine they're suited to American tastes?"

He half smiled. "I'm sure of it."

"It will do."

After a half hour, apparently satisfied with what she could find and what she had ordered, they left the market behind.

"Now is it time for a shower?" he asked.

"Oh, yes. Hot and long."

"Then I'll run home to clean up. Back later. And oh, by the way? I doubt you packed for a long stay, so feel free to use the washer and dryer."

HILLARY WAVED AS he drove away, then carried her small bag of groceries inside. Not what she had hoped for, but it would do for now.

But after she'd put everything away and had showered, time hung heavy on her hands. She wasn't used to days with nothing to do, and Trace still hadn't told her how he intended to look for Allan's killer.

A glance at the clock told her it was nowhere near local suppertime. She thought about wandering over to Melinda's bakery, wherever that was, then decided against it. After noon, bakeries had usually shut down their kitchens.

Maybe bright and early tomorrow. Besides, she didn't have the meats she wanted yet. Not that she was accustomed to having familiar meals while she was training. She'd often wondered who had invented those rations. Dried everything.

She'd also picked up some black bread that would do with the butter she'd bought. And a bag of frozen broccoli.

Some things remained the same.

She wished Trace had pointed her in some direction that she could follow, but he hadn't. She was reluctant to dive into all those papers in the office. It would feel like a trespass, an invasion. Not that there was probably much to find, other than personal stuff that was none of her business.

The solitude wasn't good for her, however. There were enough nightmare images engraved in her mind to haunt her. Hillary needed no photo to tell her what had happened to Brigid. She tried not to think about it, but silencing her brain was difficult.

She tried meditating but couldn't focus. She attempted some yoga, but that didn't help, either. Finally, she pulled on her favorite sweater, a natural-colored wool cable stitch, and waited for whatever Trace might bring.

It wasn't long before Stan Witherspoon heard that the woman was staying for a while. A friend of Brigid's.

Uneasiness crawled along his nerve endings until it became a full-blown anxiety attack. Had Brigid told her something? Mentioned it to her? Might he have as much to worry about from her as from Trace Mullen?

He felt as if a vise were closing around him. Almost suffocating him. What was he going to do about this? Wait and see?

Maybe that was the only thing he could do right now. Wait and see if the two of them started to act in some way other than as friends.

God. Sitting in Mahoney's Bar, he ordered a third boilermaker. Maybe it would settle his nerves.

He had to hope that nothing would come from this. But hope was a slender thread, and a sword hung over his head.

Chapter Five

Trace returned to Hillary as soon as he could. He had a feeling that leaving her alone in that house with all the unfamiliar ghosts it contained might not be comfortable for her.

Inevitably she had to be thinking of Brigid, and the kind of life she had lived there with Allan. Few enough answers for her in that house, in her friendship.

Sighing heavily, he wondered if he was haring off in some mad hunt to make himself feel better about Allan. Maybe Allan's despair had overwhelmed him after all.

But every fiber of Trace's being rejected that idea. What was bothering him as well now was Hillary's decision to stay. Was she just feeling sorry for him? Joining his crazy quest for Brigid's sake and not from any real belief that Allan had been killed?

Why should she believe him, anyway? She didn't know Allan well enough to feel one way or another. He almost wished he hadn't shared his suspicion with her. She had a life to get on with, people she had wanted to visit. Sun in the South of France.

He'd interrupted all that. No one else to blame for

it. Maybe he needed to attempt more forcefully to persuade her to return to her plans.

His cell rang just as he pulled up in front of the Mannerly house. It was the butcher from the supermarket.

"Tell the lady most of what she wants will be here by noon tomorrow," Ralph said. "And you might want to add the salmon is fresh with skin on."

Trace blinked. "How'd you manage that?"

"Connections."

Trace was half laughing when he approached the door and knocked. Hillary answered quickly, her face a study in sorrow.

His first thought was to divert her, possibly make her feel a bit happier. "I think you like salmon with the skin on?"

She appeared startled as she stepped back to invite him inside. "Why do you ask?"

"Because I just had a call from the butcher. Most of what you want should be here tomorrow by midday. The salmon will be fresh and have the skin."

That drew a smile from her. "That's the best way. All the good vitamins are in the fat between the skin and the flesh. But that shouldn't be a question, should it?"

"Some people don't like the taste."

She closed the door. "Then some people don't know how to cook it."

"A distinct possibility."

She led the way straight to the kitchen, and inevitably he thought of all the times Brigid or Allan had led him in the same direction, often for a bottle of beer and something salty to go with it.

He didn't find beer, but he found a fresh pot of coffee waiting. "So you're a heavy coffee drinker?"

"Any time of the day. My mother preferred tea, but I never liked it. I want a stronger, bitterer brew."

He agreed with her. Running around on a mission where you had to keep your mind clear in order to keep your head, you developed a passion for caffeine, even when the coffee was the instant kind and mixed with cold water.

And they still needed to eat. Damn, it was becoming a constant refrain for him, a desire to keep her fed because he understood her conditioning.

"You want a sub sandwich later?" he asked, wondering if they even had them in Norway.

She tilted her head. "We call them big bite sandwiches. You have them in this town?"

"Of course. The butcher makes them to order. But that's later."

Much later. The chasm still lay between them, a gulf about what they would do for Allan and whether she really wanted to join this hunt. Accustomed to walking through life with a great deal of confidence, Trace wondered why he felt such uncertainty with Hillary.

"You know," he said slowly as he filled two coffee mugs and brought them to the table, "you really should go back to your travel plans. I shouldn't have mentioned my suspicions, especially since they're probably lunacy."

Her tone took on a slight edge. "Do you think me incapable of making my own decisions?"

Trace realized he'd put his foot in it. He couldn't

blame her if she got angry. Paternalism, he'd heard someone call it.

"No, I don't think that." And why the hell was he worried about it? He shouldn't even feel guilty. It *was* her decision.

She met his gaze straightly across the table. "Do you believe your suspicion?"

"Yes."

"Then we will look together. You for Allan, me for Brigid."

Sensible enough. "Then you don't think I'm crazy?"

That pulled another half smile from her. "Time will answer that, I believe."

Bingo. "I never saw myself as Don Quixote."

"Most of us don't see ourselves as tilting at windmills, even when we are. That book may have been a comedy, but it carried a core truth—that we have to try."

He liked that. "You're right."

Again that small smile. "We tilt at windmills all the time. Even at war. *The continuation of politics by different means.*"

"Clausewitz was right," he acknowledged. "We'd like to believe otherwise, though."

"It rarely makes one feel better to look through that lens. Dealing with it is difficult enough."

She paused and he took the opportunity to speak. "The human race is political all the time."

"Hence the jobs we have. We fight because it's the only way left to settle matters. And sometimes there are good reasons for it."

He liked her clear-sightedness, her willingness to stare at reality. "I don't think much about the reasons."

She answered firmly, "Nor should we. Our countries ask, and we answer."

He sipped more of his cooling coffee. They were growing philosophical, and that would take them nowhere useful. They both wore uniforms with pride. That was the beginning and end of it.

She spoke again. "When do you have to return to duty?"

"Not for a while. I'm on medical leave. Knee injuries."

"Not good for jumping from planes." She didn't wait for a response but moved on. "Where do you want to begin this quest?"

He'd thought about it, and the truth was that he wasn't sure. He'd considered finding his way through Brigid and Allan's emails. Maybe some of the papers in their office.

"Emails," he said. "First thing that occurred to me. I'm reluctant, though. That's so personal, I hate to trespass."

"If there's a mystery behind Allan's death, I'm sure Brigid wouldn't mind. In fact, she would suggest it."

"No doubt. Still." The intimate peek into the Mannerlys' love life seemed an invasion of the worst sort. "After that, the papers and other computer files. If Allan killed himself, there had to be a reason. If someone else killed him, there was an even bigger reason."

"Then we'll start there. Do you have the passwords?"

He leaned forward. "It struck me as weird, but Allan left them to me in his will."

Her eyes widened a bit. "Then there was a reason. He wanted you to find it."

Also the beginning and end of it. Trespass he would.

THE OFFICE HAD collected some dust since Allan's death. Maybe it had started collecting even earlier. Nonetheless, even as they shook things off or wiped them down, he could still detect the faint scent of his friends.

Their journey through this world had been cut way too short. His chest tightened as memories began to rise within him. So much happiness and love simply erased.

"Before we really start," he said, "let's go for a run. I need to work off some agitation."

"I'm not surprised. Let's go." She cocked her head. "You run quite a bit for a man with bad knees."

"Two knee replacements. I'll keep working them until they stop hurting."

"Is this allowed?"

"Absolutely."

Choosing not to run in his jeans, he hurried back to his house to get his workout gear. He hated leaving Hillary alone, then gave himself a mental kick in the butt. *Valkyrie*. She could damn well handle just about anything, including the emotional turmoil that might arise. The last thing she needed, or would want, was protection.

When he returned to the house, Hillary was doing push-ups in the living room. He had to smile. Fine tuning. Answering her body's demands. Her expression appeared lighter, as if she looked forward to this run as much as he did.

Procrastination, he supposed, but both of them were engaging in it. Nor was the period they spent on a run going to deprive Allan, or Brigid, of anything. No time sensitivity there.

The day had brightened, a clear blue sky overhead. The air carried a chill that reminded him of a crisp apple. Perfect days were few and far between, but this was one of them.

He just wished his friends were here to enjoy it with him.

When they reached the top of the climb, silent agreement caused them to start down again. No running over the ridge today. The task awaiting them had begun to pressure them.

He just hoped that Hillary had been right when she said Allan had left him those passwords for a reason. Otherwise he was going to feel like a voyeur.

HILLARY COULD HAVE kept running for hours, but she was plagued by the feeling that she was running away. While she was sure Brigid would want her to look at private things, especially in light of Allan's death, that didn't make her feel any better about it.

Thinking of her own emails over the years, she was sure she wouldn't want anyone reading them. They told the story of boyfriends past, stories that got more than a bit steamy when she was away training or on a mission. A sop to loneliness that might well reveal more about herself than she'd like anyone else to know.

Painting an emotional picture of her over the years, if someone cared to piece them all together. Emails to her father, private in the way only two soldiers could share. Some things she would never want her mother to read. Tears over death in her unit. Complaints about a particularly tough training schedule, most of them in her earliest days with the Jegertroppen. She'd gotten over herself pretty quickly. One had to or would never survive.

She survived her transformation into a well-oiled cog in the machinery that served a greater cause. A growth from girl to woman to Valkyrie. A steady toughening into an elite warrior.

No, she wouldn't want anyone to read those emails. Except in this case, she, Brigid, Allan and Trace were cut from the same cloth. If anyone could approach with understanding, it would be her and Trace.

But the fact that Allan had left Trace all those passwords... The idea had left a cold feeling in her heart, a presentiment of something awful around the next corner. It was a feeling she knew well, but familiarity didn't help.

Whatever they found might shift the world off its axis.

When she and Trace got back to the house, they took turns in the shower. He'd had the foresight to bring a change of clothing with him. She had one final change in her duffel, so she decided to do a load of washing. It would keep her busy in a different way.

She was down to her camouflage, the most comfortable clothing for travel. She hoped she didn't have to wear it outside, because it would give Trace more questions to answer about her, and she'd appreciated the brevity of his introductions to people they met.

Then it could no longer be postponed. No reason to put off the inevitable. Except Trace found one.

"I'll run out and get those subs now. We can eat them whenever."

"Are you reading my mind?"

His expression remained grave. "Possibly. Shamefully, I've reached the point of being a coward."

"So have I."

She watched him take off in his car, then started another pot of coffee. Once they began, she suspected they'd keep going late into the night. Well past bedtime for her Norwegian clock.

Her days and nights had begun to sift together, though. A familiar feeling and not a bad one. At least jet lag hadn't laid her low again.

Tough it out. Across thousands of miles came her father's voice. He was a loving and kind man, but he'd never accepted half measures. *Tøff det.*

She needed to right now.

Searching the cupboard, she found steel insulated mugs with covers. Pleased, she washed two and poured the rich black coffee just as Trace returned.

"I smell the good stuff," he remarked. He placed a large paper bag on the table, a bag that appeared to be holding four long sandwiches. Beside it he placed a six-pack of beer.

"Lager, I'm afraid. I didn't know if you'd want something else."

"Lager is good."

He put it in the refrigerator along with the sandwiches. Then, with full mugs in hand, they headed toward the dreaded task.

Hillary could almost feel Brigid right behind her, urging her onward. God, she missed her friend.

HILLARY SPOKE. "Jet lag may be catching up with me once again. I'm feeling a bit chilled." She stretched and yawned. In front of her stood a stack of papers on the corner of the desk. Beside her Trace stared at computer files.

He answered, "Eight hours' time difference, right? I'd be feeling a bit chilled, too, at four thirty in the morning."

"Yes. And I'm staring at my watch and trying to believe it's eight thirty in the evening."

He chuckled quietly. "Let's give it a break. Then I'll put on my food-pusher hat and mention that we haven't eaten anything in hours."

"Food pusher?" She raised her brow.

"Well, I keep noticing how often I talk to you about food. How often I suggest that we should eat. It's starting to become weird."

She laughed. "And when you're on active duty, how much do you eat? More, I would guess, than we've been eating. Anyway, food becomes an obsession for soldiers."

That was true, he thought as they went to the kitchen. The subs still awaited them, and he brought them out.

She didn't object when he placed two bottles of beer on the table.

"I'm sorry I couldn't get fish on the sandwiches," he said.

She laughed again, a light, pleasant sound. "My obsession."

As they unwrapped sandwiches, she remarked, "We have a national dish in Norway."

"Really?"

"Really. Well loved. At the moment, there's a big argument about whether it should be changed."

"Why would anyone want to change it?"

She shrugged. "Ask the politician who started the argument. It's not like anyone has to eat it or will eat differently."

He nodded, lifting half his sandwich. He'd ordered just about everything on these subs, hoping it would tickle her fancy. "What exactly is it?"

"Boiled lamb and cabbage."

He was startled. "For real?"

"Actually quite tasty. Apart from fish, we consume a lot of lamb in Norway. Mainly because we raise a lot of it."

Boiled lamb didn't sound tasty to Trace, even with cabbage. He let it go, returning to matters at hand. "We haven't found anything."

"Not yet."

"Are you always so positive?"

She shrugged. "How negative are *you*?"

Not very, he decided. He couldn't jump into dangerous terrain without a lot of optimism. Look at his knees. He'd trashed them during a night jump on some very rough terrain overseas. And still he wanted to go back to full duty, although that didn't seem likely now.

"You get into the mountains in Afghanistan very much?" he asked, although he didn't expect an answer.

She shook her head. "You know I can't answer that."

Which told him all he needed to know. How had he not heard of the Valkyries operating in Afghanistan? He'd known Norwegian troops had participated as part of the allied operation since the beginning, but no word about a unit this unusual? Secrecy was common, but the novelty of the Valkyries must have been burning in someone, trying to burst out.

Sitting there with Hillary, he was impressed by the deep cover that had apparently shrouded the Valkyries. "You have any problem with keeping secrets in the Jegertroppen?"

She cocked an eye at him. "Last time I looked, we were human."

He laughed. And once again he was avoiding the issue of Allan. God, he needed to stiffen his spine. The grief of this task was going to tear him apart. "I don't want to do this." As sorry a statement as he'd made in his entire adult life.

Hillary didn't ask what he'd meant. "I don't, either. Brigid. What if all this somehow had to do with her?"

Trace felt her words like a jolt. She had thrown it on the table. He'd been trying to avoid thinking about that possibility. Something untoward might have happened involving Brigid, but even so, why would it have reached around the world to Allan? Why would anyone come after him?

Maybe that was the question that needed answering.

He spoke. "Allan put their emails in encrypted files. Unfortunately, he created those files all on the same date, which makes searching them difficult."

"I've found a few written letters from her. Maybe the answer is there, if I can recognize it."

"They might have communicated elliptically. Not saying it straight out."

Her sandwich done, she reached for her beer and swallowed nearly half the bottle. "That worries me."

It worried Trace, too, but they had to keep trying. Or at least he did. "If their deaths are linked, then it's a helluva problem."

AFTER THEY FINISHED their dinner, Hillary stepped outside to clear her head in the fresh, chilly air. She had a feeling that Trace wasn't going to stop for hours yet, and, despite her internal clock, she wanted to help.

She needed the time in the fresh air, though. Just a bit.

Looking up at the stars overhead, she noticed she didn't see as many or as clearly as she did while skiing and marching through mountainous terrain. Too much ambient light from streetlamps, and maybe dust.

But she clearly recalled traveling over snow, across glaciers. At night she could see many more stars than here, like a sparkling diamond coat thrown over the world.

But never had she stood under such stars thinking

about a man. Trace kept slipping into her mind, bringing warm syrup to her veins. She'd felt strong attractions before, but this was powerful. And pointless. She would be going home to her *real* life before long, job done or not. Trace would be left far behind to become only part of her memories.

Thoughts of Brigid were not far away, either. Her throat tightened, and her chest ached. So much loss. So much waste.

Determined to answer the questions Brigid would have asked about Allan's death and maybe her own, Hillary turned and walked back into the house. Sleep and fatigue had become irrelevant.

So THE WOMAN was moving in, Witherspoon saw as he watched. Brigid's friend, the grapevine said. Why was she staying? Hadn't her visit to the cemetery been enough? Or was she getting sweet on Mullen? It was possible. Women were often drawn like moths when it came to men like him. Strong, hardened, dangerous.

Or maybe it was something worse. Because Mullen had been quite convinced that Allan's death wasn't suicide and had made no secret of his belief. Damn him. Mullen should have accepted the decision of the cops and the inquest. Despite his protests, they had listened to him and then ignored him.

After the determination of suicide, Stan had hung around to make sure it was over. He *had* to make sure, because a mistake could cost him his life.

But since this woman's arrival, he couldn't stop sweating it. No matter how many times he told himself it was too late, that nothing further would be done, he couldn't escape the sense of threat, no matter how many boilermakers he put away.

Brigid had seen him twice. He'd had her killed. When the hammer didn't fall on him, Witherspoon had decided she hadn't reported up the chain of command. Hadn't caused trouble for his boss. Until the man told him to take care of Brigid's husband. The boss must have heard something.

Stan had been all over this ground so many times his head ached from the unending spiral of his worries. Sometimes he wondered if he wasn't going a bit mad over all this.

Then had come Brigid's friend. A friend close enough that she'd come all the way to visit a grave.

Well, he'd worried constantly that the boss was right about the husband. He'd taken care of that. Now he was worried that Brigid had mentioned the matter to her friend.

God! His worries just kept getting stronger. They were beginning to overwhelm him. Mad or not, he wondered if he'd be able to think through this clearly, to figure it all out to his advantage. His brain seemed to have escaped him.

He felt like a rat in a maze, unsure which way to turn. He didn't want to kill again. That seemed like hanging his butt out too far into the breeze.

He kept telling himself that if Brigid had talked to anyone, he himself might be dead by now. But no one would consider her report important enough for her to be killed. Except him. Hell, if she'd reported it, who would really listen? One woman, a couple of sightings of something she knew nothing about.

He'd made that argument to himself countless times.

But he was getting lost in the maze, unsure how much he was lying to himself. He'd been afraid enough to kill two people. Now a third?

Were money and a hazy threat really that important?

Well, it had gone past money. It was racing toward jail or possibly his own death. He *had* to tie up loose ends. He couldn't risk any ends to unraveling.

He had become a man wandering in a warren, hiding in bushes, losing his marbles. He had come to that.

Hell.

TRACE TRIED TO shut it down for the night. He knew what an eight-hour jump in time zones could feel like. But Hillary refused to go to bed.

She was determined to glue herself to his side and help him. He figured, given who she was, that she had at least as much determination as he did. No backing down. An argument was pointless.

Besides, he didn't want to argue with her. After her shower, the aromas of shampoo and soap had clung to her, and the enticing scent kept distracting him.

Trouble there, he reminded himself. Big trouble. Plus, she was Brigid's friend, and he didn't want to do the least little thing to offend her.

His own shower had disturbed him. Allan's shampoo. Allan's bar soap. Familiar scents. At least Hillary must have brought her own things. He might have gone nuts if he'd smelled Brigid as well as Allan.

There was nothing more evocative than smells, as he knew from shooting at the gun range outside town. The smell of burned powder could sometimes throw him back into battlefields he'd left behind. Bring a resurgence of memories that should be erasable.

He sighed, rubbing his forehead. Maybe he needed some glasses for this job. His eyes were growing tired.

He glanced at the time and saw it was nearly midnight. Nearly 8:00 a.m. in Norway. Her body must already have awoken to a new day.

"Are you going to bed?" he asked. "You need some sleep."

"I'm wide-awake."

"I was afraid you'd say that."

"You can go sleep if you want to. I can continue here, and for you it is late."

He smiled. "It's rumored. I'm fine. Maybe a little caffeine to help."

"Sounds good," she answered, her eyes on the papers she was sorting through. "I'm making a pile of Brigid's handwritten letters to go through when I'm finished. Odd that she wrote letters as well as emails."

"Good idea." He paused, studying her, with an unending curiosity about her that seemed to be growing. Little things. Maybe later some big things. "Do you ever get worried about avalanches? Or blocks breaking off glaciers and falling on you?"

She shook her head a little and glanced at him. "We are well trained to look out for the dangers. If we make a mistake—well, we get what we deserve." She shrugged.

He shared the same kind of training, although not

about glaciers. It had been a dopey question, he supposed, but it had probably sprung from his fogged brain. Time to make that coffee or give up and go to bed. Since she'd already worked her way through her own fatigue to help him, he wasn't going to leave her working on her own. Besides, it wouldn't be the first time he'd sacrificed sleep to a mission.

And this had become a mission in the truest sense.

Chapter Six

In the morning, although worn out from the long night, Hillary and Trace took off for a run. Each strike of her foot invigorated Hillary, as did the fresh morning air. The rhythmic movement was also soothing, calming. A lot of tension began to drain from her.

Thinking about their search for a clue, she wondered if it would yield anything truly useful. Yes, she believed Allan had left his passwords to Trace for a reason, but that didn't mean the documents would have anything at all to do with his death. Or Brigid's, which was probably an even crazier thought. A rocket-propelled grenade had killed Brigid during a mission in dangerous territory. Easy enough to understand in the circumstances.

Even if they found anything useful, it wouldn't change the inquest verdict. Trace must be doing this for his own peace of mind, niggled by the concern that maybe Allan *had* died by suicide. Or maybe to find a killer. Allan's killer.

Of course he would want that. She fully understood. But with only emails and handwritten letters, they probably wouldn't find any kind of description of the murderer, even if he existed.

Hell! And now this situation had made her worry about Brigid's death. Now she couldn't stop, couldn't just say she needed to get back. Now *she* had a powerful need to know when before she hadn't even wondered about it.

She wished she hadn't thought of the linkage between the two deaths, at least not in the way she had. Were the deaths related? Probably, but most likely only because Allan had despaired after losing Brigid. That *was* the most sensible explanation.

When they reached the top of the ridge, she wanted to stay there. To continue this brief rest away from their self-imposed task. To maybe think very seriously about returning to Europe and resuming her interrupted plans.

Not that she would. She'd made a commitment here and she honestly didn't regret it, even if it turned out to be a waste of time. There was something to be said for paying full attention to the death of a friend, to settling with oneself before returning to daily life. Even finding nothing at all could bring a measure of peace.

Or maybe they would tumble into some information that recorded the details of Allan's descent into despair. The part of him he'd probably kept to himself even while expressing it through alcohol. Trace wouldn't like to discover that. He'd hate it. But at least then he wouldn't have to wonder.

As they approached the outskirts of town, she saw a man standing beside the road. Young and slender, maybe thirty or so. With an unshaven face, as was so popular. Dark hair.

He stared at them as they approached and passed, and she felt a tremor of unease. When they had left him behind, with the Mannerly house just ahead, she wondered aloud, "Why was he staring at us?"

"Maybe because he's never seen two lunatics running like this without being chased by an angry bull."

Amused, she chuckled. But the sense of uneasiness had taken hold and she couldn't help looking back. In the distance, the man was walking away. He'd probably decided he'd had his entertainment for the day.

"Let's grab some breakfast," Trace suggested.

She didn't argue. It had been twelve hours or more since that sandwich had filled her, and right now she could do with a bit of sweet pastry, or whatever passed for it at the truck stop.

She needn't have wondered. She hadn't looked closely at the menu before, but now she turned to the back side of the four pages. The sweets were clustered on the back of the menu, a good selection. And down at the bottom was oatmeal, nearly invisible.

At the top, beside a stack of doughnuts, was something labeled Danish pastry, although it looked to her like Viennese bread. Whatever the name, she liked the pastry.

Now she had a breakfast that would do. A double order of oatmeal and two pastries. Plenty of carbohydrates.

When their food arrived, Trace spoke. "You looked a little troubled when we were up top."

"Just thinking about what we're doing. If we'll get any satisfaction." She didn't mention she'd thought about going home. He might try to send her on her way again, and there was no point growing irritated with him.

He grew serious, putting his fork down. "I know we might be wasting time. We might find out that there was no murder. That I was wrong."

She ached for him. He had been plowing alone through a painful emotional abyss. "But you need to know anyway. At this point, so do I." She reached for a piece of the so-called Danish. The delicious, sweet, flaky pastry pleased her.

"I admit," she said presently, "that it was easier to accept Brigid's death when I thought it was the result of ordinary combat. A common attack from insurgents. Now I feel unable to accept it."

He finished a bite of toast. "Exactly."

They shared a look of understanding, and Hillary experienced the first real camaraderie with him.

A while later he asked, "What are you going to do with that salmon you wanted?"

"Try to remember how to cook it."

That caused him to laugh. She liked the crinkles around his stormy gray eyes when he did so.

"You're invited," she said. "You might even enjoy it."

He nodded. "Thanks. Anything you need me to bring?"

"Yourself. I'll have to think about anything in addition."

"Think away." But as they approached the house

once again, he said, "That man we passed really bothered you, didn't he?"

"Yes," she admitted. "Battle sense, I suppose. It can get overactive at times."

"Maybe."

At least he hadn't tried to dismiss the observer again. Uneasiness still clung to her like cold, wet leaves. Somehow that just hadn't been right.

She dreaded spending another day in those mountains of paper. Hours of inactivity looking through items, including utility bills, that probably had no relevance at all. Her friend hadn't spent a lot of time making files.

She might have sighed, but she didn't want Trace to hear it. It was difficult to appear impassive all the time so that he wouldn't feel guilty about her decision to stay.

Commitment. It meant as much to her as duty and loyalty. She *had* committed herself of her own free will.

THAT MAN HAD bothered Trace, too. A small thing. Maybe the guy had been gawking only because it was rare to see a man and a woman running in step around here. Different leg lengths usually would have made that difficult, especially about being in step, but as he had remarked, in a unit not every leg length was the same. They had all learned to adjust their strides to the same length.

Hillary was tall. How many times had she adjusted her stride when the soldiers ran as a unit? She had a hell of a lot of experience doing it.

After their showers, Trace began to feel angry.

"What the hell happened, Allan? What is this all about? Another reason to drive me mad?"

Hillary looked at him, clearly a bit astonished, then said quietly, "I share your frustration."

"I bet you do. Neither of us is inclined to sit on our butts for endless hours. We need activity. Action. But I'm not going to get truths out there running my behind off. Left to my own devices, I'd probably be doing that run twice or more a day. Do you people ever run such distances twice a day?"

"Depends. For conditioning, yes, sometimes."

"Then we start feeling the lack of all the rest of it." He wiped a hand over his face. "I'm going to buy more beer, or something else. Any preferences?"

"Pilsner, if your stores carry it. It's what I drink mostly at home."

"I'm sure I can find it. Anything else?"

She tilted her head, as if considering. "Aquavit is excellent."

"I'll get some if it's available. We might need a few shots before this day is over."

She hesitated then stood. "If you can wait a moment or two, I'll go with you." She didn't want to make any kind of splash in this town, to get noticed too often. It went against her training and instincts. But he was right about needing activity.

"I'll wait. I'd really like the company."

Teamwork. They were both used to it. And being covert in strange places.

This time she allowed her sigh to escape. He was

right about the inactivity. Before long they were going to feel like prisoners in this house.

TRACE RENTED A room by the week at a gracious house on Front Street. He ran in to get a change of clothing but didn't take long. He'd never tried to rent a place long term because he was so rarely in town. A room was plenty, and Brigid and Allan had often made their tiny guest room available to him.

For nights when they'd drunk a little too much at the kitchen table. For nights when they'd been having so much fun that it had startled them to realize it was nearing dawn.

God, he missed them both. Brigid's death had nearly gutted him. Allan's had finished the job. So he'd sit on his butt to make sure that neither of them had come afoul of someone or something.

It was nice, however, to come back to his SUV with Hillary. A comrade. A companion. Another soldier. Someone who understood.

But the more he dug into his suspicions, the emptier the horizon appeared.

Man, he was sick of spinning his wheels. Allan's death hung over him like a dark cloud, almost suffocating. Crying out for a resolution. Any kind of resolution that convinced Trace more than the inquest had.

Yeah, Allan *could* have died by suicide. He'd faced that much even if it had flown in the face of Allan's nature and his words. Allan would never surrender, even though Trace had been worried about his drinking. But what if he had?

Then Trace would have to learn to live with it.

The liquor store sold both pilsner and aquavit, the latter surprising him in such a small store. He'd often wanted to try it, but just in case he didn't like it, he bought a bottle of bourbon for himself.

When they exited with their paper bags, the breeze had escalated into a cold wind. Winter's breath forced itself down his neck like sharp needles. Not long and the snow would start falling.

As they strode toward his vehicle, he nearly paused. Wasn't that the man who had been watching them from the road earlier? Some instinct warned him not to make a misstep or to look with more than a casual glance.

Who the hell was it? Over the years he'd gotten to know nearly all the longtime residents around here, but there were still new people he'd never met, mostly from the community college.

He slid into his truck next to Hillary, and she said, "Did you see him?"

"The guy? I did. I also couldn't be sure it was the same man. I didn't look hard enough."

"Me either, but he troubles me."

Situational awareness. Drilled into him bone-deep by training and experience. Sometimes it just paid to be on high alert.

"DAMN IT, ALLAN," Trace grumbled several hours later. "My butt is killing me from sitting in this chair. I *have* to move around."

Hillary apparently agreed. She rose and bent over to stretch her glutes and hamstrings. Next were her shoulders, then she shook her arms as if to release the last tension. His moves weren't very different.

"You'd think," Trace groused, "that he could have labeled the folders somehow. But worse, the emails inside them aren't in chronological order. Like he took a mixer to them."

Hillary nodded as they strode toward the kitchen.

"I used to love this room," he remarked. "Good times in here. Now it feels... I dunno. Annoying? Like a prison? Confining. God!"

When he'd thought about starting this search, he hadn't thought about turning into a library rat. Stuck in a chair for hours on end. Those two had emailed each other at least once a day, sometimes more, and the emails went back for years.

"I tried a search," he told Hillary as he made yet another pot of coffee. Then, changing his mind, he got a couple of beers out of the fridge, giving her a pilsner. "The damn search algorithm won't go by dates on the emails."

"Frustrating," she agreed. She began pacing through the house, evidently as tired of sitting as he was.

Much as he had avoided the living room, he could avoid it no longer. The empty space where Allan had once sat wrenched him. The rest of the room was familiar, now feeling too familiar. Stuffed with good memories, now drowned by ugliness beyond words. But hell, he'd deal with it.

Maybe he was crazy now, but he'd been crazy for the last two months with the conviction Allan hadn't killed himself. He was going at the problem the only way he could think to do.

And it was nuts. They could spend a week going through all this and find nothing. There had to be a better way.

Hillary stopped pacing when they returned to the kitchen, and she sipped more of her beer. "Allan mixed them up for a reason."

"I already figured that out. But if he was so damn worried about something in there, why didn't he share with me? With anyone? And then leave me all his passwords in a *will*?"

"We agreed it was some kind of message."

"Yeah, but what kind?"

Her lips quirked. "Did you expect to parachute in and conduct a quick reconnaissance?"

At last he relaxed enough to laugh. "Too impatient, huh?"

Hillary shrugged. "Perhaps. And perhaps you haven't considered how dangerous this could be."

"I have, actually." He waved a hand. "If Brigid and Allan are linked, if both were murdered, then we've got a huge problem by the tail. Especially if word gets out what we're doing here."

She half smiled. "So maybe it's best you haven't told anyone I'm a soldier, too. Just being Brigid's friend may bring enough attention."

True. Once again he thought of that guy in the parking lot and alongside the road. Had he been watching? Or was it coincidence?

She spoke, reaching beyond the anger that drove him.

"Brigid was killed by an RPG. At least according to the after-action report."

Trace looked at her. "And so it ends?"

"If anything was going on, yes."

His spine stiffened. "Do you know what you're suggesting?"

"Oh yes." He watched as her face hardened. "It's impossible anymore to know who fired a shot. Too many US weapons out there among insurgents. Too many Soviet weapons out there. The RPG was probably US." Her face darkened even more.

"Are you thinking friendly fire?" he asked.

"I cannot ignore any possibility. Not now."

That was one thought that hadn't occurred to him, mainly because Brigid's death out there shouldn't be linked with Allan's here. *Shouldn't.* But maybe it was. They'd both realized that possibility yesterday.

"God, I'm starting to feel stupid," he remarked. "Maybe it's time to start thinking like the warriors we are and throw emotion out the window. At least me. I've been letting it govern me too much."

"That's understandable. I have had longer to get used to Brigid's death. To grieve her."

At three that afternoon, before they could discuss only the barest bones of new ideas, a knock at the door surprised Trace.

"Nobody's stopping by here anymore," he remarked as he went to answer it.

It proved to be Deputy Guy Redwing, an acquaintance of Trace's. A man in his early thirties, his face carried a hint of Native American heritage. "Hey, man," Trace said. "What can I do you for?"

Redwing smiled. "Just a check. This house hasn't stirred since Allan died, and now it's busy. And no one recognizes the woman who's here. Put it down to nosy neighbors, but I gotta answer the call."

"Yeah, I know. Come on in. You might as well meet Hillary and put everyone's mind to rest."

Hillary had come to the kitchen door and was smiling. "Coffee?"

"Yes, ma'am."

"Then come along. I'll make some."

Redwing made the same comment Trace had made upon meeting Hillary. "You sound kinda English."

"Kind of," Hillary agreed, offering no more. "I was Brigid's friend."

"It's all a sad, sad story," Redwing said. "I'm Guy Redwing, by the way."

"Hillary Kristiansen. Nice to meet you."

Guy settled at the table while the coffeepot burbled and steamed. "Neighbors around here are nosy. You'll have to get used to it, I'm afraid. Everyone's looking after everyone else most of the time. And then there's times like this when it's none of their business but they still want to know."

Hillary laughed. "I lived in a town like that."

"Then you understand."

Trace poured coffee for Guy and brought it to the table. "Is it still getting colder out there?"

"Enough that I can see my breath." Guy turned his

cup around a few times before taking a sip. "I'm not trying to stir anything up, but Trace knows I grew up here."

Trace replied, "Just a couple of years behind me."

Redwing chuckled. "You guys were always my heroes back then."

"Why the hell?" Trace asked. "We were just like everyone else."

"Except the three of you always knew what you were going to do. Wear a uniform. I guess I got mine."

"A good one, too." Trace grinned. "So how's it going?"

"Sometimes busy, sometimes not. That Grace Hall investigation was something else. Imagine someone trying to drive her off her land and killing to do it."

Then Redwing eyed Trace. "I don't think it was suicide, either."

A pin drop would have been deafening. Breaths grew louder in the quiet that seemed to fill the room. Not one muscle twitched among any of them.

Trace eventually cleared his throat. "You don't?"

Redwing shook his head. "Never could stomach it, despite the inquest. I knew Allan. I talked to him more than once after Brigid was killed. Messed up? Yeah. But determined as hell to get through it. A matter of honor, I thought. And maybe for Brigid."

Trace nodded then drummed his fingers. "But nothing specific, I suppose."

"If there had been, the inquest wouldn't have ruled it a suicide. But I've never believed that."

Trace unleashed a pent-up breath. "Everyone else does."

"I doubt it," Guy answered, "but what's the point of saying anything? The inquest settled it, and not many people want to argue with their neighbors or look like fools, either."

Trace and Hillary exchanged glances.

"Then," Guy continued. It was his turn to sigh. "Seems like Allan thought there was something fishy about Brigid's death. But what the hell was he going to do about it? That happened thousands of miles away. Enemy fire. Why didn't that ever sit quite right with him?"

"I don't know," Trace answered slowly.

"Anyway, it was just a feeling I got." Guy smiled faintly. "I wasn't going to shout about it the way you did. Not without decent evidence."

"I was freaking mad. Angry."

Guy sipped his coffee again. "It sucks," he said frankly.

Trace leaned forward, forgotten beer bottle in front of him. "Did you notice anything at all? Maybe some stranger acting oddly?"

Guy's expression turned wry. "Maybe you haven't noticed because you're away so much, but every summer and fall we get a new wave of students. Even faculty can change. No one sticks out, not with that college here. Besides, a whole lot of them act odd."

Trace smiled. God, he needed the humor, and his smile broadened when he heard Hillary laugh quietly. "I acted oddly at that age, too."

"Didn't we all?" Guy asked. "I suspect marijuana causes some of it, but so far we haven't detected signs of stronger drugs. The sheriff isn't exactly worried about personal quantities of marijuana, though."

"What's the point? He'd probably have to arrest half the students at the college. And maybe a bunch of high schoolers."

Guy chuckled. "It's becoming legal through use."

Once again silence fell. Hillary went to get the pot to heat up Guy's coffee. "Thanks," he said. "I can tell you, Trace, I'll keep my ear to the ground. Or the vine. Whatever."

She put the pot back and returned to the table. Guy looked at her.

"You're pretty quiet," he remarked. "You knew Brigid, though?"

Trace felt her tense beside him. He couldn't blame her for not wanting everyone to know she was a soldier, too. But maybe some things had to be revealed to put a lid on speculation.

"They met in the war," he said, leaving it at that.

Guy pressed no further. "Then I'm doubly sorry," was all he said.

But Hillary was evidently prepared to share some things. "We grew close very fast. Brigid showed me a locket she never took off. Inside it was a photo of Allan."

Trace hadn't heard that before. In fact, he hadn't known about it at all. Apparently the Mannerlys had had a few secrets, even from their best friend.

"That's sad," Guy said. "I mean now. Not at the time."

Hillary nodded. "At the time, I was touched that she shared it with me."

"Did it survive?" Guy asked.

"No," she answered. Very little of Brigid had survived, but she wasn't going to tell these men that she'd been identified only by DNA. No one wanted to hear that.

After a bit, Guy stirred. "Back to duty, I suppose. I'll tell the neighbors there's nothing going on here, that Hillary is just Brigid's friend. Maybe that'll shut down the gossip."

Maybe, thought Trace as he watched Guy drive away. But then they'd find something else to speculate about. Like why Trace was practically living here with Hillary.

The curse of small towns.

WITHERSPOON WATCHED GUY REDWING drive away. The tension in his neck was beginning to strangle him. Law enforcement? What had those two found out?

Maybe it was time to just pack up and go. Get out of here in case those two *did* discover something. Pretend he'd never found evidence of it. Would the boss believe him?

But how could it lead to *him*? He'd been banging his head on that wall ever since this had begun. Had Brigid discovered his name somehow? If so, had she repeated it to anyone?

Damn. But if she had, the rock fall of her revelation would surely have landed on his head. Stan Witherspoon would even now be facing a trial. Or would have been murdered at the hands of the man who had hatched the scheme. As far as Witherspoon knew, however, the big guy hadn't discovered Stan's fears.

It wasn't that Witherspoon was alone in his misdeeds. Plenty of contractor equipment got diverted, stolen or just never shipped at all. A military contract meant money, and more money if the company could find a way to cheat.

Stan was only a small part of the problem, a man they would leave alone unless someone raised a ruckus. Then the higher echelons, having known this was going on all the time, would want to make an example.

Either way, Witherspoon would find himself in a vise that might be fatal.

No, he had to make sure he was never discovered, that no one linked to him was discovered. Especially now that he'd committed two murders.

He probably should never have done it. Never let fear and threats guide his actions. All he had now were more serious problems.

But fear drove him, and fear didn't yield to reason.

Chapter Seven

Trace looked at Hillary. "What did you think?"

"Guy seems like a nice man."

He snorted. "You know what I mean."

"I could use a shot of the aquavit, if you don't mind."

He glanced at his watch. "Late enough for me."

"And I need to try to cook a supper for us. I don't want that salmon to spoil."

"Hillary…"

She smiled. "I know. I'm being difficult."

Difficult didn't begin to cover it.

"I found dried dill in the cupboard," she remarked. "Fresh dill wasn't available at the market, but dry will do. There are bread crumbs here, too. In this house, someone cooked."

Trace had to smile. "Maybe I just wasn't here when it happened."

"It's likely. You were more fun."

He shook his head once. "I haven't been fun lately."

She didn't answer, just brought the aquavit to the table. "Do you want your bourbon?"

"I'll try yours first." He rose and went to the cabinet

where Brigid and Allan had kept the shot glasses. He rinsed and dried two of them, then placed them on the table while she peeled off the seal and opened the bottle.

Then she poured two shots of clear liquid, saying, "I believe this label is infused with caraway. Others may have a dill undertone, or possibly other herbs."

"Do you like this one?"

"I like caraway. It's just a hint, but you will probably taste it. No surprises."

He had to smile as she joined him. "So it's not vodka."

"It may look like it, but it is made mostly from grain and isn't as strong as some vodkas."

She regarded him over the shot glass. "In the summer many of us drink beer. In the winter, more aquavit. Maybe it helps with the long, dark nights."

He laughed. "Makes sense."

"We are a sensible people," she answered wryly.

He thought more about her home country and what little he knew about it. "You have a border with Russia?"

She nodded. "It is a difficult border. Mountainous, of course, but also too porous. We share part of the North Atlantic oil field with Russia, mostly in the North Sea but not entirely. That means we must patrol with our navy also." Then she downed her shot of aquavit.

It appeared to go down easily, so he tried his. It surprised him with its viscosity. "That's good."

"As to the border, we train to defend it, although we judge the likelihood of Russian invasion to be small. But it makes our NATO neighbors feel more comfortable."

"Do *you* train for defending the border as well?"

"We train in the mountains," was her only answer.

Good enough, he supposed. He drained another shot. "I like this."

"Have another."

He was agreeable. Other than running, having a drink was the most pleasant thing he'd done recently. Too focused on Allan. It was a wonder he had any friends left, and he wasn't too sure about that.

She turned the conversation back. "As to Guy Redwing, well, he surprised me."

"Me too. I've been feeling pretty much alone since the inquest. I had no idea that anyone didn't think I'd gone nuts."

"I don't think you are nuts. You have legitimate questions about what happened."

"And no evidence."

He poured himself another drink. He liked the caraway undertone to it. And a hint of something else he couldn't identify. "I wonder if he'll learn anything."

"I don't know. He hasn't learned it yet. But perhaps he'll look harder now."

Trace wondered about that, then his mind wandered back to that man they'd seen twice. It might be odd; it might be nothing at all. Now he wished he'd taken a closer look.

"That man," he said.

"Yes. It seemed strange, but this is a small town. No reason to think it wasn't just coincidence."

No reason at all except that uneasy crawling along his neck that often warned him he was being watched.

She spoke. "We might find something in those papers and emails. Allan seemed to think them important."

"He must have known I'd be reluctant to go through them, though." But the passwords. He kept coming back to them. "Hell. Spending all our time in that office is uncomfortable."

"We will just keep running."

That almost made him laugh. Running from what? A boring and endless task?

"Is it your dinnertime?" she asked after a while.

"I'm flexible."

"We have to be, don't we? But I need something to do."

He could sure understand that. "I suggest a walk around town tonight. Maybe folks will talk with us."

"At least out of curiosity."

"That much, anyway." He watched as she preheated the oven and spread a large piece of foil on a baking pan. Then she took the fish from the fridge and placed it skin side down on the foil. Next came quite a bit of dried dill and some fresh lemon juice. Over the top she sprinkled bread crumbs. At last she wrapped it all in the foil.

"Looks good," he said.

"Even the dill?" she teased.

"Even the dill."

"Now I need something to go with this. The fish won't take long, maybe eighteen to twenty minutes, but anything else might take longer."

"I thought you didn't know how to cook."

She laughed. "This I think I can remember."

Her laugh was such a pleasant sound, filling the kitchen in a way he very much liked. Some kind of cheer needed to return to this house. To his heart.

"This house needs two ovens."

That startled him. "Why?"

"Because I bought frozen french fries. I didn't want to peel and slice potatoes. And the frozen fries take a different temperature than the fish."

"Oh, the problems."

She laughed again. Activity seemed to make her happier. He watched as she brought broccoli from the freezer. "This will do in the microwave. I hope you like buttered dark bread."

Hillary was making his mouth water. "Now I'm starving."

That pleased her. From out of nowhere, a desire to please her *all* the time struck him. *No go*, he reminded himself. Soon she'd be thousands of miles away again.

HILLARY HADN'T COOKED dinner in a while, although she'd misled Trace a bit. When she and her father were home at the same time, she often cooked, and she enjoyed doing it now. Scents wafting from the oven made her homesick and brought back good memories.

The wooden cabin where they lived together, by no means small, with a steeply sloped roof so snow would fall off. The nearby village, brightly lit in the long, dark nights. Welcoming.

The nights that lasted three months were among her favorite things about her home. Even having lived there all their lives, some grew irritable before the end of the darkness. Not Hillary. Those days were a time for gathering with friends when she wasn't on duty. For sitting beside a dancing fire on the hearth.

After supper, they headed out for their walk, bundled up against the icy night.

Trace spoke. "That was the most delicious dinner I've had in a while."

"I'm not surprised," she answered drily.

He laughed. "Where do you live in relation to the Arctic Circle?"

"North of it."

"Kinda cold and dark. I'm not sure I'd like it."

"I do."

"Why doesn't that surprise me?" he joked.

"Because I haven't moved south?"

"How would I know? I have no idea where you started."

The weather hadn't grown cold enough yet to drive the evening crowds indoors. Freitag's Mercantile was still open with plenty of customers. She had liked shopping in there.

People greeted Trace as they walked, and he seemed surprised. "I guess I've been too obsessive about Allan to think anyone wanted to speak to me anymore."

Curious looks came Hillary's way, but only a handful paused to talk to them. To them, Trace introduced her as Brigid's friend.

Everyone expressed their sorrow at Brigid's passing, often with a nice memory of her. Hillary got the feeling they had truly liked her.

But some also mentioned Allan. Those that did

seemed reluctant to bring him up, as if they knew that Trace still wasn't convinced it was suicide. And among them were people who said they didn't believe it was suicide, either.

"Damn shame," said one man. "A blot on his memory, and I don't think Allan deserves that. He was tough enough to get through anything, including the death of his wife."

Trace nodded, refraining from reiterating his opinion. Hillary imagined he thought they already knew it. He must have made quite the uproar.

Apparently the instant the seeds of suspicion had been planted in Trace, they'd grown fast and sturdy. Suspicions always did. But she had begun to believe he was right. The only difficulty was solving the problem.

Trace spoke to a few more people, and more than one said they thought he was right. It appeared both Allan and Trace had some good friends in this town. They'd stand by Trace no matter what.

Hillary spoke, thinking of good friends as they turned back in the direction of the Mannerly house. "My father was often away, so I had a nanny." The memory came with easy grief. "She has been gone for years, but she was good to me and became my friend. I always wondered why my father did not marry her. Then as I got older, I realized Pa didn't spend enough time at home to grow another love inside himself."

"Our lives are much the same."

She scanned the street continuously, a habit learned from being in the military. Always know your surroundings, where people are, where buildings are, what's the best cover or escape route. Even here in this quiet town it wasn't something she could quit doing.

And with her awareness came a subtle tension.

Then she saw the man again. He might be trying to be invisible, but the way he held his head... It was him.

She kept walking but said quietly, "You see him?"

"Yes."

Matters were rapidly growing more interesting. And making her just a bit concerned.

"OKAY," TRACE SAID when they got back to the house. "I've got to find out who he is. Twice could be coincidence, but three times?" Tension coiled him tight as a spring.

He looked at Hillary and saw her nod. She said, "It's not likely even in a small town."

"You feeling hunted?"

"Yes."

"Damn it!" He didn't bother to moderate his voice. Along with the tension came anger, a lot of anger. "But if he's trouble, I have to be careful about how I poke around."

"Are you trained to gather intelligence of this kind?"

"Like this? Not exactly."

"Neither am I. My training focused on urban interface and gathering intelligence from women."

He lifted a brow. "Why women?"

"Because they will talk more freely with another woman."

"I can see that," he admitted. "Especially in some

regions of the world where a woman can be killed for talking with a strange male."

"Yes." Then she shook her head again. "I feel this could get bad."

So did he. That feeling of being hunted was all too real to ignore. He'd felt that way more than once when on a mission, but never before in this town.

"Hell," he said, expressing his anger once again. When he looked at Hillary, he saw a spark in her gaze. Anger? Maybe. She'd lost Brigid, after all. And he didn't think a Valkyrie was feeling nervous. Nope.

They spent a long night going through files and papers. Trace kept feeling he was on the cusp of a discovery, but it eluded him. Once again he felt seriously annoyed by the way Allan had mixed all this up. No question but that he'd been trying to conceal something.

A small stack of handwritten letters grew beside Hillary. All the envelopes had been opened, but she didn't pull out the letters. Not yet.

She *did* say, as she had thought already, "It's odd that they handwrote so many letters. In these days, email has replaced that."

"Yeah. Let's leave them, though, until you finish sorting. If the letters contain something, it might be easier to fit all the pieces when we look at them in sequence. Which is more than I can do with these files."

He sighed and got back to work, convinced all over again that Allan had wanted him to find something. But what?

Chapter Eight

The next afternoon, after some sleep, they were interrupted several times. Trace was surprised as relationships that he'd ignored began to knit themselves back together. Evidently he was being welcomed back into the fold.

But where had these people been during the inquest, or right after? Had they been hoping for a different decision? Or maybe Guy had been right. They didn't want to look like fools in front of their neighbors.

Among the flow of people who stopped by, claiming they wanted to see how Trace was doing, came one who surprised him because they'd been acquaintances but never close.

Edith Jasper, a woman who might have been in her late sixties or early seventies, stopped by with her harlequin Great Dane, Bailey. A frail-looking woman, everyone wondered how she handled that dog. She managed, considering that she and the dog could not be parted. Nor had Edith ever suffered an injury.

Bailey's huge head reached above Edith's waist, and Trace was sure the dog would totally dwarf her if he stood on his hind legs, but Bailey was also polite. He had what Edith called *house manners*. He leaped on no one, but when he sat and grinned, he still looked gigantic.

Trace invited them both in, and after introductions he watched Hillary fall in love with the dog. She knelt on the floor, Bailey sat down and the two of them immediately began to cuddle.

"Well, that's the seal of approval," Edith remarked.

Trace smiled. "Can I get you something, Edith?"

"It's cold out there, but Bailey needs his walks. Anything hot or warm will do, thank you."

Hillary looked up. "There's an unopened bottle of cider in the kitchen closet. Warm it up with a cinnamon stick."

Trace went to follow orders. Behind him he heard Hillary laugh and Edith chuckle.

Later, as they settled in the living room with hot cider, the subject of Allan and Brigid came up.

"I liked them both, have since I taught them in seventh grade," Edith said. "A very pleasant young couple, and they seemed truly happy together. At least when they *were* together." Then she frowned at Trace. "Do you know that I wanted to see you ever since Allan died? Only you were too busy chasing your own tail. When I was out and about, you'd always vanished somewhere."

Trace nodded. "I guess so. I did a lot of running."

"Eating those miles up. Like I do with Bailey. Dog keeps me young and healthy."

"And he doesn't give you any trouble?" Hillary asked.

"Not a bit. Folks used to worry that he'd pull me off my feet, but he's never tugged once. It's like he senses I'd wind up on the pavement."

"He is an angel," Hillary replied.

On the floor, Bailey lay with his head between his front paws, but it was clear neither his nose nor his eyes were missing a thing.

"When angels start visiting me," Edith answered, "I'll begin to worry."

She turned again to Trace. "About Allan."

Trace felt his shoulders begin to tighten. His stomach started feeling like a hollow pit. Again. "Yeah?"

"He was a good man. One of the best. But I was concerned about him after Brigid died."

"He was drinking a lot," Trace remarked, his voice heavy.

"But not that much. Too much, but not enough to make him stagger."

"You think he was depressed?"

"Of course he was depressed," Edith said sharply. "Who wouldn't be? But it wasn't his drinking that bothered me. That's just a man's way of dealing with too much emotion." She cocked a brow at Trace. "Men need to learn how to cry."

He smiled faintly. "Maybe so. But about Allan?"

"Yes, Allan. He was ripped up, but he'd have come through it. And you insisting it couldn't be suicide. Unless I'm sorely mistaken, that man didn't have quit in him."

Trace tensed even more. "I don't think he did."

"A lot of people heard you. Made everybody a little nervous about what you might do."

"As in?"

"Ripping this town apart from end to end."

Hillary smiled faintly but said nothing.

Edith continued. "Then you went into that shell and didn't seem to see anyone. Folks stepped back. Didn't want to disturb you."

Trace frowned. "Not a pretty picture, Edith. Did I make you feel that way?"

"Not about ripping the town apart. I've known you since I taught you math. I figured you wouldn't even put your fist through a window. Too sensible."

"I hope so."

Edith nodded, appearing satisfied. "I was right. Seventy-odd years have taught me a few things about human nature. Anyway, I wondered if you were right about Allan."

Trace drummed his fingers on the arm of the chair. He was growing impatient, feeling as if Edith might know something. If so, she had a roundabout way of getting to it.

Edith sipped more cider. "Regardless, my old brain began to rattle around in my head. It does that every so often, and when it does things pop out, useful or not. I suspect Allan wasn't just grieving Brigid. He was bothered by something."

Jolted, Trace leaned forward, resting his elbows on his knees, thinking about those passwords. "By what?"

"I wish I knew. He never said, and I guess he never

told you. It was just a feeling I got. I can't be sure, Trace. Just a sense."

Edith set her cup aside and rose. "I've got to get Bailey back to his walk before he starts whining like a baby."

She started toward the door, Trace accompanying her. Before she stepped out, she looked up at him. "I really am inclined to believe he didn't commit suicide. Period."

After Trace closed the door, he discovered Hillary right behind him. She looked uneasy.

"What do you think?" she asked.

"That Edith might be right. But we already considered the possibility."

"I know. But she validated it."

Trace closed his eyes briefly, thinking over what Edith had said. She had only a sense that Allan had been troubled by something other than grief. But her sense was good enough for him.

"Let's go for a run," he suggested. "I need to work out all this tension. You?"

"I'm always ready. Then we'll dive in again."

Hillary was clearly hooked.

THE MOUNTAINTOP WAS PEACEFUL. After stretching, Hillary sat on a boulder and looked down at the town below. Brigid's death had been bad enough, but this growing belief that it might have been murder was twisting her insides into knots.

That someone might have plotted to kill Brigid

seemed impossible, but the impossible now stared her in the face, growing more possible by the minute.

Her sorrow deepened. What had always felt like a waste now grew into something bigger. She looked at Trace and thought about his fight against the idea that Allan had died by suicide. About the intensity of his drive for months.

Now she felt the same intensity. Edith's words had stamped the need into her heart. If it was murder, Brigid must be avenged. Anger twisted around her grief, stronger than it had been in the immediate aftermath.

She noticed the shadows were deepening, warning of the approach of early night. She rose, stretching a few times, then said, "Let's go before we stiffen."

Not that Trace had been likely to do that. While she'd been sitting morosely on a rock, he'd kept moving.

She ran faster than before on the downslope, taking a big risk on the rutted track. She needed that risk, needed to feel her head clear, needed the adrenaline rush that came from danger.

Trace, on the parallel rut, kept pace with her. Not a word about this being hazardous on such uneven ground. The dirt before her was pitted, full of rocks, utterly uneven. She knew she was foolish to do this without a threat chasing her, but she didn't care, relying on her boots to protect her ankles.

The pounding of her feet on the ground felt almost like the rage pounding inside her. A Pandora's box had opened inside her, unleashing the Valkyrie, the hunter.

She wanted a battle.

TRACE SENSED THE shift in Hillary. He couldn't glance at her until they reached level road, but then he did. It was a wonder she hadn't bared her teeth.

In that instant he saw the warrior inside her, the one she kept beneath a carefully controlled exterior. As they all had to do, but this was his first true introduction to the woman within. The Valkyrie.

He'd seen that expression on the face of other soldiers going into battle. During battle.

As they approached the end of their rapid run, they both breathed heavily. He still managed to ask, "Are you going to start a war?"

Her blue eyes looked icy. "Against who?"

That was the problem for them both. No idea where to direct all this rage, all this angry sorrow. They were shadowboxing.

They went home without seeing that guy, leaving Trace to consider the possibility that they'd both over-reacted. He had mixed feelings about that. He wanted a person to focus on but doubted that would be likely. Not after all this time, unless the killer lived in this town. Which, given what Edith had said, seemed extremely unlikely.

Rage, like a banked fire, burned within him.

What the hell, Allan?

LATER, HILLARY INTRODUCED Trace to a "Norwegian breakfast" that felt more like a supper to Trace. It had consisted of slices of the hard sausage the butcher had ordered for her, small cubes of Jarlsberg cheese and thick, crunchy crackers.

"That's breakfast, huh?" he asked as they headed back to the office.

She shrugged one shoulder. "Most of us prefer not to eat breakfast at all. You will have a hard time finding any café or restaurant that is open to serve breakfast. We tend to have what you call brunch."

"I liked it."

She smiled. "You should consider yourself special. That was a buffet style, which is found in hotels."

"I'm honored."

Her smile turned into a laugh as she took her seat at her side of the desk. When she looked at the stacks of paper, her smile faded, however, and her face turned grim. "Trace?"

"Yeah?"

"I may go mad if we don't find something soon."

"Me too." He had begun to drag the scattered emails into folders by date, most recent first. Initially, it had made him squirm to peek into the love that had flowed electronically between them. Made him feel like a voyeur. Anger had burned out that concern.

He understood why Allan had opened all this to his scrutiny, however. He doubted that Allan had trusted anyone else to read this intimacy.

"Damn it, Allan, give me a clue!" He only realized he had spoken aloud when Hillary made a sound. He turned to look directly at her. "Sorry."

"Go ahead, Trace. I feel the same way, and I may soon be cursing Brigid."

"Maybe it would do us some good to have a minor temper tantrum, stomping our feet and yelling."

She laughed outright, her face clearing. "I didn't think of that. I was wishing for a punching bag."

"Better idea. Maybe we can get over to the high school gym and pound them."

"Make it a date."

Date? Trace wondered how she had meant that. A flicker of hope sprouted inside him, but he tried to stomp it out. He didn't want to disrespect her with a one-night stand kind of thing.

He glanced at her from the corner of his eye. Unless that was her style?

Ah, hell, he thought. His mind and body usually bent to his will better than this. But with her so close, her feminine scents enticing him, it was difficult. He'd have liked to escape into her for a few hours. To discover once again one of life's greatest beauties. To drag himself, and her, out of this ugly swamp they'd walked into.

After he felt he'd moved all the recent emails into one file and was once again on the edge of going stir-crazy, he found something. His heart sped up.

"Hillary?"

"Mmm?"

"Take a look at this. It's not much."

She scooted her chair over and peered over his shoulder. "Where?"

Stuck in the middle of some graphic prose, Allan had written, *Let it go, sweetheart. Just let it go.*

Hillary read the email twice before saying, "That doesn't fit. It is out of place."

"It might mean almost anything. Maybe a small squabble."

"But it doesn't belong there."

He passed his hand over his face. "No, it doesn't." Allan was worrying about something. But Trace felt it like a sharp prod. His determination revived, he leaned over the computer again. "Let's keep going. Whatever it is, Allan tried to bury it."

He checked the date again on the email. He'd been out of town. Maybe Allan hadn't wanted to share the issue, or maybe he'd forgotten all about it.

Or maybe he'd been too worried to speak about it.

"When was that email sent?" Hillary asked.

"Mid-January."

"Brigid died in late January." Her frown deepened. "Too close."

"I agree."

Something had been going on. Something bad enough to get Brigid killed? Out there that wasn't impossible. Life began to feel cheap.

Hillary spoke. "It wouldn't be the first time someone out there has been killed for no reason."

He knew exactly what she meant. "When you pull the cork out of that bottle, it can splash anywhere."

"Good analogy."

"But this time it sounds like there might have been a reason."

"It does." Her face impassive, she turned back to the stack of letters she'd been compiling. "Maybe it's time to actually read some of this."

Hours later, they called it quits. The night had grown deep, settling into silence except for the sound of a cold wind whistling around corners and through tiny cracks.

"Banshee," Hillary remarked.

"Are you trying to give me chills?"

A smile leavened her face. "I doubt you ever get chills."

"Neither do you, except possibly when it's forty below."

Her smile became a laugh. "I would like aquavit. You?"

"It might help get us some sleep."

If nothing else, weariness lessened the pressure. There was just so long a person could stay wound up. As Hillary walked to the kitchen, she rotated her shoulders, trying to ease the tightness in them. She was definitely unaccustomed to spending so many hours at a desk.

The laugh had felt good. Brief as it was, it had unknotted her stomach a bit. She was on the hunt now, deeply involved. That one line in Allan's email seemed heavy with portent. Dark. She'd known Brigid well, and her friend wasn't one who needed to be told to *forget it* over a disagreement.

Brigid had had a good soul, part of what had drawn Hillary to her. How that soul had survived combat operations, survived risking her neck to escort convoys, survived having to fight, Hillary didn't know.

Her own soul had suffered cracks. She knew she wasn't as forgiving as Brigid had been. Hillary was less ready. She was quick to dismiss someone as an idiot. Or even as evil in an extreme case. She was also quicker to remember, to not forget.

Her feeling was that when a snake bit you, you shouldn't go back to playing with the snake.

Brigid had walked this earth lightly.

As she sat across from Trace with aquavit, she said, "Brigid was a bright soul. Was she always like that?"

One corner of his mouth lifted. "Frustratingly sometimes. She wouldn't let you get a good mad on. *Forget it* was one of her favorite phrases. The other was, *Is it important enough to waste your energy on?*"

Hillary nodded, remembering Brigid saying just that. "I admired that in her. I am not so good."

"Me neither."

Hillary slipped briefly into memory, then returned. "Allan. He was like her?"

"They were kind of yin and yang. He was… I don't know how to describe it. He was a lot more reserved. He was harder. You know what I mean."

She did. Then a stark thought occurred to her. "That phrase that leaped out of Allan's email?"

His gaze grew intent.

"Allan was harder, you said, but he tossed those words back at her. Maybe it wasn't a reminder. Maybe it was a warning."

Trace tossed back the last of his aquavit. "Hell. I'm awake now. I'm going back to work."

Hillary waited just long enough to brew another pot of coffee. Then she followed him with two insulated mugs.

The hunter inside her had fully roused, and she was on the trail. She would not be deterred.

As MORNING BEGAN to creep into the cold world, Trace looked at Hillary. She looked back. Fatigue was written on her face, a slight draining of color, but she sat upright, her posture firm. This woman would keep going until she dropped into a coma.

So would he, probably, but they would quickly become useless. "Operational readiness requires at least some sleep. We both know that." They both parted to go to their separate rooms. Hillary found it difficult to sleep and wondered if she had just grown too tired. A paradox she had faced before.

Closing her eyes, she wandered her memories of Brigid. They hadn't spent a whole lot of time together, as their missions were different and Hillary didn't spend long periods at the rear base, although for a while she had visited frequently.

Regardless, their friendship had happened almost explosively. Hillary might never understand how it had happened so fast. It just had.

Brigid was a dark-haired woman with sherry-colored eyes that seemed to glow from within. She smiled most of the time and appeared to be surrounded by good buddies of all genders.

But somehow Hillary had leaped into the inner circle. To become someone in whom she could confide, who could confide in her. Even about the locket Brigid kept concealed inside her uniform. A secret.

For the first time, Hillary wondered just how many secrets Brigid had guarded.

Hillary rolled over and hugged the other pillow.

She hadn't done that since before she joined the Jegertroppen, partly because there was never an extra pillow, and partly because it might be interpreted as softness. Or childishness.

She didn't know who she was angrier at—Brigid, because she might have involved herself in a matter that had gotten her killed, or the person who might have arranged it.

As she hugged the pillow, other thoughts trailed in, mostly thoughts about Trace. He appealed to her on so many levels. Men outside the special forces never really understood, and there was much she couldn't share.

Trace crossed those boundaries. She didn't have to explain, because he knew.

He was sexy as hell. She wasn't immune. She'd seen the glint of attraction on his face, but something kept pulling him back, maybe the same thing that kept pulling *her* back. The distance that would soon lie between them. Half a world.

She liked him, too. Her practiced impassivity wasn't too deep for that. Inside her there was also a woman like any other.

And she wasn't afraid of fleeting sexual relationships. She'd had a few before. She was the one, usually, who ensured they were fleeting. Giving her heart might be a very stupid thing to do, so she kept it, clinging tightly to it.

But this would be different. She wouldn't have to fight her way out or think of a million reasons for leaving. Trace already knew that was coming.

Maybe, she thought. Warmth filled her just by thinking about it. A warmth full of desire. Of heat.

She drifted away to sleep at last, thinking about Trace.

Outside, in the frigid wee hours, through slight slits in a couple of curtains, Witherspoon watched the lights turn out at last.

Bundled up against the cold, he thought he resembled one of those puffy cartoon characters found in an ad. Given the temperature out here, he doubted anyone would notice his gear, but they might notice him standing in the yard behind bushes.

Yet he needed to move on before he froze to death. He'd been out here too long, giving serious thought to breaking into that house while the two of them slept and taking them out.

Except that taking out two people was a lot more difficult than taking out one. Whoever he shot first, the other was going to come after him. They were both soldiers. He'd heard that late last night in the bar. He knew all about Trace Mullen, about his Airborne background. That man could be serious trouble.

But a female soldier, according to gossip about her being in the war? He'd never seen them as a serious threat.

Maybe, just maybe, he could take out Mullen first, then the woman. Hell, she might have been nothing but a glorified paper pusher.

But still. He had enough sense left to consider two murders to be a dangerous proposition. Enough sense to turn away and walk back to the student apartment he rented. Enough sense to get home before he turned into an icicle.

If the woman went back to wherever she came from,

the problem would be halved. He needed to add that to his planning before he did something he'd truly regret.

He regretted killing Allan Mannerly. Still, the whispers around town suggested that Mullen still didn't believe it was suicide. And now the whispers suggested that a whole lot of people in this town were questioning it, too.

They might have zipped their lips for a while, but they were not zipping them anymore.

That frightened Witherspoon as well. Too many people were shifting positions for reasons he didn't know.

What the hell was going on?

Once again he thought of moving out, but the mess he might be leaving behind could come back to kill him.

He was getting to the point of wanting to tear his own hair out. He'd bitten his fingernails to bloody nubs, and now he was chewing his lower lip raw. Making his teeth hurt from grinding them constantly.

Brigid Mannerly and her husband had gotten the easy part of all this, he decided. An easy, fast death.

Witherspoon feared he would not be as lucky.

Chapter Nine

Two days later, Hillary glanced to her right as she headed for the bathroom. Trace sat on the edge of his narrow bed, a towel wrapped around his waist, displaying a rather respectable six-pack as he pulled a shirt over his head.

But what she most noticed were the black neoprene knee stabilizers. Given that he never complained about his new knees, she was a little surprised to see those stabilizers. Regardless, he put a lot of tough miles on his legs. He should have been reaching for paracetamol or ibuprofen, but she had never seen him reach for a thing. Tough guy. Not giving an inch.

Without a word, she grabbed a large blue knapsack she'd found in the bedroom closet. So he wouldn't wonder, she left a brief note.

Then she headed to the grocery, determined to remember how to cook well enough that they didn't need to go out again. She'd never really liked dining out except with a group of friends. Besides, she wanted some different flavors.

She filled her cart with vegetables and fruit. She was

unable to resist the bananas, which must have traveled a very long way, and six fresh, crunchy apples fell into her cart. Amazing, she thought with amusement. As if they might have jumped right in.

She wasn't a heavy beef eater, but a really impressive steak looked back at her from the cold case. She bet Trace would like that. In fact, he might even have a preferred way of preparing it. That joined the stack in her cart.

Her shopping list got longer as she went, until she nearly laughed at herself. She must have been craving some things without realizing it.

She was, however, happy to see Trace come through the door just as she was ready to check out. She knew she had chosen too much to fit in the knapsack and decided it would be easier to carry the rest with help. Grocery bags could have a mind of their own, even with handles. She wished for the net bags she'd used at home.

He smiled when he saw her. "Looks like you picked up a lot. Hungry?"

"For something different."

"Mind?" He looked through her cart. "Well, I have to confess I can read a recipe. If we can get some potatoes, I'll brown them in the oven. Do you like rice?"

"Brown rice."

"Coming up." He also brought a few mixes that looked like they'd provide some muffins or loaves. "We need our carbs."

Very true.

"Are these real bratwursts?" she asked as they passed down the meat aisle again.

"They're American bratwurst. I don't know how that compares to what you're used to."

"I'll find out." She watched him put two gallons of milk into the cart, along with chocolate syrup.

When they left the store, Hillary realized the break had refreshed her. Surprisingly, she looked forward to getting into the kitchen.

Something besides poring over the files and letters. Two days and they'd found nothing more. She suspected they might already have gone too far back in time. "We need to run through those emails and letters again."

"Start to finish," he agreed. "Man, how elliptical can you get?"

"Quite a bit, it seems."

"Or worse, that whatever it was, they may have Skyped it."

She sighed. "That's a possibility. So now we have to find if there are copies."

"Probably in one of those damn random files I haven't gotten to yet. If Allan saved them." Then he shook his head. "I have to keep reminding myself that Allan wanted me to find something."

"Maybe he hid it too well."

Trace snorted. "He may have. Some idea of what I'm looking for would be a great help."

"You didn't see him before he died?"

"I didn't get here for Brigid's funeral. I was on a mission. Then I was in the hospital and rehabilitation, under medical control until they decided I'd recovered enough to be turned loose. By then I only had a month with him before…" He shook his head as they pulled into the driveway.

She mulled that over as they carried the groceries inside. Only a month with Allan before he died and no secrets shared.

At times she faced the sacrifices demanded by her career, but she preferred not to think about them. It did her no good to focus on selfish desires.

Putting the groceries away, which had originally seemed like a distraction, now felt like another delay. They had to find something so they could really get started on their search.

She took an apple back to the office with her. Trace followed with a banana. There was a chance they had missed something.

Because if Allan had become aware of a problem, it must have happened before Brigid died. Before he'd written that telltale *Forget about it*.

She and Trace exchanged looks before they dived back in. In Trace's eyes she saw a steel she felt within herself. He'd spend years on this if he had to. She didn't have that much time. It didn't help that English was more of a second language to her, despite her mother, despite English being spoken by so many the world over. It remained a second language.

Trace spoke. "It occurs to me, dunce that I am, that when I was here, Allan may not have shared the secret because he didn't want to put me in danger."

Hillary drew a breath. "I would believe it."

Then she reached for a letter and slipped it out of the

envelope for a second reading. She hoped she would find something she had missed.

An hour later she felt a small bubble of excitement. "Trace?"

"Hmm?"

"She writes of there being too many American weapons in the hands of insurgents. *Too many* is underlined."

He swiveled his chair and leaned toward her. "Show me."

He scanned Brigid's writing. Then he looked at Hillary. "You're right. It has something to do with weapons."

"That could well be dangerous information."

"Depends on why she said it. But the way she underlined…" His voice trailed off. Then he said, "I think we may have found a clue."

TRACE WAS AWARE that there was a black market in weapons. A lot of money could be made on a single M4 carbine and some ammo. Or either model M203 grenade launchers, again, if the grenades could be sold with them. The M4 was particularly versatile, as it could be mounted on the grenade launchers for added firepower.

"Hell!" He knew it happened, but rarely did anyone get caught diverting the weapons. However, if Brigid had obtained specific information about a person or organization, she might have become expendable.

Another look at Hillary told him she shared his thoughts. Trace felt sickened. Bad enough to redirect arms for money, but worse to consider a woman disposable if she learned about it.

This is what had worried Allan. No question.

He stood up. "Time for a run."

He didn't ask, and Hillary simply stood up.

Run it off, man. Run it off.

THEY PUSHED HARD on their way up the mountainside and they went farther this time, following the ATV tracks over the ridge. A bit of snow had settled up there overnight, a light dusting like confectioners' sugar.

"Winter's close," he remarked.

"Too close."

He wondered what she had meant by that. Her words hadn't sounded casual, but instead freighted with meaning.

They turned to run back down, but this time followed a slower pace, one that allowed them to talk as they ran.

"She had to have found out more," Trace said.

"I feel the same. Now we need to find out what it was. Someone must have been afraid of her."

"Maybe." Or maybe just a dyed-in-the-wool psychopath who shoved any obstacle aside without remorse.

It didn't matter what kind of enemy Brigid and Allan had faced. Trace was determined to put an end to whoever they were.

THE STEADY HAMMER of their feet relaxed them physically, but Hillary felt no easing of the stress that had grown in her after finding those words in Brigid's letter. Nothing more than that, but a strong hint. Now she was truly eager to get back to work.

She suspected Trace felt the same. Her desire to find

the person or persons who might be involved in this not only brought out the hunter in her. It brought out the soldier who would never give up, never surrender.

When they got back to the house, they ransacked the refrigerator and cupboards for something quick to eat while they worked. Another pot of coffee brewed.

"Later," Trace said, "I want to make some of those brownies I bought. I don't know about you, but chocolate is practically a medicine."

Trace had bought some thinly sliced ham that morning, and they built thick sandwiches with ham and Jarlsberg cheese.

"This is a Norwegian cheese," she remarked.

"Better in Norway, I bet."

She gave him only the attempt of a smile she wasn't feeling. "Depends on what you're used to."

"Very generous of you."

Plates and cups in hand, they headed back to the office.

Neither of them could have stopped now unless dragged away by wild horses.

They began their search again, looking for some further indication of what had happened. A name. A description of what she had seen. Somehow Allan had known.

But when you were in a combat zone, you couldn't bring your personal cell phone or computer. Everything went through protected military equipment. No truly private email or phone call or Skype.

Hence the great caution the two had displayed.

A COUPLE OF hours later, they took a break. Muscles had knotted bent over keyboards and letters, exacerbated by the pressure of finding an answer.

They sat in the kitchen over beers talking in spurts, mostly generalities. After a bit, they grew serious again.

"This whole thing doesn't make sense," Trace remarked. "One person couldn't have enough evidence to threaten any corporation. God, they've got enough lawyers to tie up the matter in court for years. What could Brigid have discovered that would be enough to threaten them, anyway?"

"It had to have been something important," Hillary agreed. The cold beer bottle sweat, making her fingertips wet. "It's a long way to go to come this far to kill Allan."

"Exactly. Silencing Brigid might make perverse sense, given she was probably an eyewitness, but Allan? I doubt much in her letters would constitute any kind of real evidence. Hearsay, probably."

"He had told her to forget it. He wasn't inclined to pursue the matter."

"But who would know that? If he decided her death was a direct result of her knowledge, then he might have been pursuing the matter on his own."

She nodded. "This problem is growing bigger. If we are right, what can we do about it?"

His gaze grew steely again. "I need to know for *me*. Even if I can't do damn all about it."

Hillary understood, but she also understood that the clue had drawn him in deeper. He wasn't stopping. He wanted much more than knowing.

She tapped her bottle with her fingertips, considering the entire situation from another perspective.

Then she spoke, a chill trickling down her spine. "We haven't considered the army itself."

"How so?" He stared at her.

"If someone up her chain of command was involved, he'd have a lot more to lose than a corporation would."

He closed his eyes briefly. "Yeah. And some officer or NCO would have a much longer reach. A lot of friends here and abroad. Hell."

"It could be like tumbling dominoes, revealing people higher in the command."

"And with each step upward, the danger would grow." Trace swore again.

THE HOURS HAD bled together. Neither of them thought of the clock, or the time difference that had affected Hillary at first. Their awareness of time was only that they wouldn't run at night. Either of them could be injured by a stumble or fall, Trace's knees especially.

But because the hours had flowed together, it was no surprise when Trace suddenly announced, "It's time to cook something. My banana has long since vanished."

In response, Hillary's stomach growled, making them both laugh.

First they spent some time in the living room working out kinks. Stretching, push-ups, sit-ups, lunges, twists…everything to loosen up and quiet muscles that needed to work.

Trace enjoyed having someone alongside him as they did calisthenics. Even more, he enjoyed the view of

Hillary in a T-shirt and exercise shorts. Such long, perfectly shaped, athletic legs. A guy would like to have those legs wrapped around him.

When they got to jumping jacks, they faced each other with an added benefit. Hillary had enough breasts to bounce a little. He figured she wouldn't like his repeated glances at all, but she *was* sexy.

But he thought she looked faintly amused, as if she knew.

A couple of times he suspected she might be regarding him the same way, but he couldn't be sure.

They traded on quick showers and a change into warmer clothes before returning to the kitchen, where beer sounded better to them both than another pot of coffee.

Hillary studied him, looking less impassive than usual. "That scar on your cheek? Do you mind telling me?"

He shrugged. "A knife."

She didn't ask how, which was fine by him. Thinking about the war wasn't going to give either of them the break they needed.

"Dinner," she said, changing the topic. "Any preferences? You helped put it all away, so you can't claim ignorance."

He smiled. "No excuses. Well, I was eyeing that steak. I can't cook it on the grill in this weather, but I *do* remember how to cook a steak in a frying pan. What else?"

She considered. "Vegetables. And perhaps those frozen fried potatoes?"

"Oh yeah. And maybe I'll make some of those dang brownies." He wiggled his brows at her. "I'm pretty sure I can follow the directions on the box."

"I think you would be very good at following directions."

"Oh, I like the sound of that."

She laughed. "You would."

She had flirted with him. Unmistakably. He liked it, but it ratcheted his desire for her to a whole new level. Looking at her now, he wondered if her reserve was cracking.

Not that he'd been opening up very much. He'd been taking his private trips down memory lane, but he hadn't shared them. Keeping an emotional distance. Why should he expect anything else from her?

The war. It hovered over everything. The endless war that was steadily becoming the modern version of the Hundred Years' War.

He got out the thick steak, nicely marbled. Hillary pulled out the frozen veggies and fries. Together they calculated cooking times.

"As best we can," Hillary laughed. "Two rusty cooks. What do you think we'll make of this?"

"If I ruin that steak, I'll never forgive myself." He flashed a grin, surprised that it was coming so easily. Some of the somberness and anger had faded, at least for now.

"You brighten this place up," he said as he stabbed the steak repeatedly with a knife and spread butter all over it.

"What are you doing?" she asked.

"My dad always made them this way. Good browning and some buttery flavor throughout."

She poured vegetables into a glass bowl. "French fries in the oven first, I think." She pointed at the package. "I can follow directions as well."

Again. Damn, his groin was beginning to feel heavy with hunger. He forced his attention back to the steak.

"What did you mean, I'm brightening this place?" she asked.

"This house. It's so full of memories of Allan and Brigid that at first I could barely stand to be in here. Now, well, you're changing that. This house was never intended to be a mausoleum."

Her voice softened. "I think it was intended to be a haven for wounded hearts."

"And a happy one. They made the most out of every moment they were together. Made the most of our friendship, too." Forgetting the steak for a moment, he stared into space, remembering all the laughter, all the joy. When those two had been here, they'd shed everything that might have haunted them.

"Haven," he said, returning his attention to finding a frying pan while Hillary spread the fries on a baking sheet and popped them into the oven. "That's a good word for it, Hillary. A truly good word. It was a healing place."

"Maybe that was the reason they wanted you to have this house."

He hadn't thought of it that way. Instead he'd seen it as a dark place full of grief. As a place haunted by people he had loved who were now gone. A repository of good memories that could only bring pain.

"Maybe so. I sure couldn't imagine why they wanted to give it to me."

"Perhaps because they weren't the only ones who were happy here." Having closed the oven and set a timer, she said, "Flip in eight minutes. I can manage that."

That drew a laugh from him. "Like there's very much you can't manage. Should we go out back and build a fire with twigs?"

She joined his laughter. "That's easy."

"I was afraid you'd say that. I'll have to think of something more difficult."

Later, as he was frying the steak, she asked, "Do you have family here?"

"None. Mom died giving birth to me. My dad raised me, then skipped out right after I left for the Army. I have no idea where he is."

She fell briefly silent. "That's sad. Maybe he felt he couldn't risk losing you, too."

"I don't know. I didn't see him that way, but I could be wrong. He was always taciturn and strict. No-nonsense. I turned to my friends. He steadily turned away." He paused. "Sometimes I wondered if he blamed me. If he looked at me and got angry or something."

She didn't answer. *What answer could there be?* he wondered. No one could know.

But then she offered, "It's awful you felt that way."

He shrugged. "It was what it was. A fact of life. I

didn't concentrate on it—I just built my own life. What about you?"

"What about me?" The timer dinged, and she pulled the fries out, beginning to turn them over.

"Your mom, your dad. That couldn't have been easy for you."

"It wasn't especially difficult. I didn't have to wonder if they both loved me."

"And your dad?"

She smiled as she placed the fries back in the oven. "My best friend. We talk about everything." Her smile grew softer. "I have so many images of him, sometimes stern, but mostly with his eyes crinkled in a smile for me."

"It would be easy to smile at you."

She glanced at him, seeming to hold her breath, but only for a second. "That is a very nice thing to say."

"It's just true. How did you grow up?"

"When my father was home, we did nearly everything together. Long ski trips in the mountains, some camping, some traveling, sometimes just sitting by the fire and talking with friends. Many good times."

He had never known that himself, but the image she painted was warm and inviting. He could almost picture it.

He pulled the steak out of the frying pan. "We're doing pretty good," he remarked as the microwave beeped that the vegetables were done. A minute later, the oven timer went off.

She tossed him a glance over her shoulder. "Just the way a military operation *should* go."

"But never does."

"Never," she agreed.

Trace had grown more comfortable with the dishes in the cupboard, so he pulled them out and set the table for them. Icy bottles of beer accompanied the settings, and then the food.

"Damn, it smells good," he said.

They sat facing each other. Trace had cut the steak in half as best he could and put a portion on her plate. After that it was every man or woman for him or herself.

"I forgot to make those brownies," he said.

"Thus failing to prove you can follow directions."

Damn, she made him laugh. At long last when he sensed Brigid and Allan in this house, he felt as if they were smiling at him.

Chapter Ten

Stan Witherspoon's fears continued to grow. The longer that blonde woman stayed in town, the more worried he became. A soldier. One who had been Brigid's friend.

On the one hand, he was glad of this town's busy grapevine. On the other, he worried that it might expose *him* in some way.

There was no way to shut the gossip down. None. He just had to continue trying to remain unremarkable.

Although unremarkable was his general description. He blended better than a potted plant.

Sometimes he liked his inherent invisibility. Sometimes he hated it. He sure hadn't been invisible those two times Brigid Mannerly had spied him at his avocation. He preferred that term, *avocation*, to the real one: arms merchant.

Hell, he'd been moving weapons for years, a cog in the chain between manufacturers and the battlefield. What he'd begun to do for money really wasn't that different. Or so he told himself.

He knew it could get him in some serious trouble,

especially with the man who had been running the operation and maybe others.

A lot could happen between leaving manufacturing plants and arriving at destinations. Even shipments of socks turned up missing, and the security on weapons didn't seem to be much more stringent. At least not when you knew what to do.

He even had heard of weapons and ammo disappearing from stateside military bases. Amazing the power of a soldier working in such a place. A little here, a little there, and a small cover-up and no one would notice.

For a while, at any rate. Didn't anyone do inventory?

A stupid question. When the guy diverting the stuff was the same one who was doing the inventory, the cover-up was easy.

As well he knew. That's why he'd been selected for this operation.

Which had brought him here. The only place that was more back of the beyond than Conard City was the place he had come from. Now he'd committed a murder in both places and was thinking about another one or two.

Had anyone asked him five years ago if he would do any of this, he'd have sworn he never would.

Until the money was offered. Until the fear took over.

He was a changed man.

He hated to think about it.

LAST NIGHT, TRACE BELIEVED, something had almost happened between him and Hillary. A look, an atmosphere, something. There had been a huge ground shift between them. Like an earthquake.

But nothing had come from it, probably because they were both cautious. Any kind of relationship would be fraught with problems.

He felt almost guilty for entertaining such ideas, given all that had happened. Well, guilt never did a damn bit of good. His mind was going to rove wherever it chose, and maybe it needed a serious break.

"We've got a lot to think about," he said to Hillary as they finished up their run. "A few threads to weave together."

"We certainly need more information to act on. Are you growing satisfied, though?"

He thought about it. "I'm growing even more convinced that Allan didn't die by suicide."

"I thought you were already convinced."

He shook his head. "There's always a doubt when you have little but belief. Now I feel justification ahead. Maybe."

The lack of answers aggravated the hell out of him. "Brigid had to have known something important. Allan wouldn't worry over nothing."

"She must have told him somehow."

"Which is why we're on this quest. And I'm sick of jawing over the same ground."

Hillary remained quiet as they slowed into a cooldown walk. Then she spoke the obvious.

"It's already clear something was being concealed."

The endless hamster wheel, Trace thought. *Totally endless at this point.* But Allan had evidently felt that Trace could figure it out.

"Hell," he said aloud. "I was never good at puzzles. Allan knew that."

"I imagine he believed otherwise. At any point after Brigid died, he could have written it all down for you to find."

"So what was he afraid of at that point?"

"Dragging you into danger."

Trace looked up at the sky. It was darkening again, pregnant with clouds. As they were.

HILLARY STEERED THEM to Maude's diner. Trace needed another break whether he knew it or not. Something to divert him a bit longer from his search. Obsession was rarely a good thing and could become blinding.

"You know," she remarked, "I have no idea what time of day it is anymore."

That drew a laugh from him. "Did we ever have? After a while in the military, you need a watch just to tell you the time wherever we are."

"Very true."

Trace glanced at *his* watch. "It's past noon and well before dinner hour. Maude's shouldn't be too packed."

Nor was it, which suited Hillary fine. They chose a table at the back. One that allowed them to keep their backs to the wall. Hillary felt inwardly amused. Soldiers. Guard the back at all times.

Maude didn't even ask if they wanted coffee. It slammed down in front of them, along with a couple of glistening menus. "Keep them tanks full," she grumped before stalking away.

Hillary and Trace exchanged looks. Trace shrugged. "I guess everyone has noticed how much running we do."

"It would seem so."

"You don't always have to come with me."

"I'd need a broken ankle to stop me," she answered. "I'm still wondering about your knees, however."

"They'll be fine." He paused. "I'm expecting notification that I'm being discharged as medically unfit, injury in the line of duty."

Hillary caught her breath. "No!" It was a sharp whisper.

He eyed her grimly. "I'll never jump again."

"That is terrible." She felt an ache for him.

"Yeah. But everyone has an expiration date. I believe I've reached mine. What good would I be except standing post at a forward-fire base?"

Maude appeared, demanding their orders. Hillary let Trace handle it because now her mouth felt as dry as sand and any appetite she'd had was gone. He'd just shared that he was facing another catastrophe on top of the deaths of his two best friends.

And this *was* a tragedy. He was confronting losing his identity, one he'd carried for many years. The day would come for her, too, as it came for everyone, but she couldn't stand to think about the day when she'd no longer be Jegertroppen. That was who she was. Eventually it would be in the past, and she'd be a *former*. A *retired*. Which wasn't the same at all.

Easy enough for someone else to say, *Well, you're other things, too.*

Except this was different. It was bone-deep different. Everything in her life had been built around this one thing. To lose it would leave her feeling gutted. She wondered if there was any way to prepare for it.

She also wondered if Trace had been trying to prepare himself, or if he'd been living on strands of hope. *"Jeg synes sind på deg."*

He looked at her and she caught herself. English. "I feel bad for you."

One corner of his mouth lifted. "It sounded better in Norwegian." Then he shook his head. "Don't. It comes to us all."

"That doesn't mean it's easy."

"Well, no," he admitted just as Maude slammed plates in front of them.

Maude said, "Everybody's talking about how much running you two do. Seems crazy to me, but to each their own. Eat. You can't be that skinny from running and not need to top your tank."

Something between a snort and a laugh escaped Trace. "Thanks, Maude."

The woman sniffed as she marched away.

Hillary looked at the mound of food in front of them.

"She wasn't joking," Trace said. "Except nobody is going to run very soon after this much food."

A laugh escaped Hillary. "I wasn't planning to do it all over again too soon."

Everything was hot and fresh, and they both dived in with pleasure. "What will you do?" Hillary asked, referring to what he'd said about disability retirement.

"When I'm tromping the streets as a civilian again?

I don't know. I guess I should start thinking about it soon. But it can't involve a desk."

The wry way he said it brought another smile to her face.

"I think I've learned that for sure," Trace continued. "No long periods at a desk. I'll have to dig up some other skills."

"I believe you probably already have them. Or you can develop them soon."

The problem was, Hillary realized, that she was not feeling those cheerful words at all. She couldn't imagine the gaping hole *this* was going to drill into Trace. She hoped he heard something different from the Army, but she feared he was right. Cogs had to work correctly or they were replaced.

"I could teach you to ski," she said suddenly.

That brought a grin to his face. "Norwegian spec ops?"

She shrugged a shoulder. "At least you could work out all that energy skiing cross-country. I don't think it would be terribly hard on your knees. And you could always teach younger soldiers."

"What they already know," he said dryly. "Thanks, but you'll have to do better than that."

She laughed. "You're right. Well, we could teach you to raise sheep."

What was she doing? she wondered. Picturing him in Norway? Oh, this was getting dangerous, and not the kind of danger she was trained to handle.

Together they walked down the street toward the Mannerly house, carrying plastic bags full of leftovers.

Maude had been more than generous, and any thought of cooking later had vanished.

For which they were probably both grateful, Hillary thought with amusement.

Since it was blustery out, few people they passed did more than say hello before moving on. Fine by Hillary. The cold was beginning to bite her cheeks, and she wished she had chosen a balaclava instead of a watch cap. But then, she hadn't planned to stay for long.

The last autumn leaves were being ripped from the trees as they strode along the sidewalk. They didn't linger long enough to cover grass.

"Have you ever wondered," she asked, "where the leaves go when the wind carries them away?"

"Into some unfortunate neighbor's lawn," he answered. "I imagine it's like the snow. Usually it blows away until it gets caught somewhere. If you're lucky, it won't be on your driveway."

She felt her cold cheeks crack into a smile.

"Say," he said as they approached the house.

"Yes?"

"I've noticed you never say you're sorry in the way we use it. As in, 'I'm sorry something bad happened to you.' Is there a reason?"

"In Norway, at least," she answered, "to say we're sorry is not an expression of commiseration. It's an apology for having done something. A statement of taking responsibility for an action."

He was quiet a moment. "That's interesting. I never thought about it."

"Why would you? It's different in English."

"It also makes sense to me. You're right, *sorry* sounds more like an apology if you think about it. I wonder if it changes an individual's perception."

"I can't say. I just know I am not in the habit of apologizing for what I can't control."

"Do you hear it the same way in English?" he asked as they turned onto the short walkway to the front door.

"I've grown accustomed to the English usage. It doesn't confuse me."

He looked at her as he opened the door. "I don't think very much confuses you."

Then, out of her came a truly American phrase. "Wanna bet?"

He broke up at that and was still laughing as they carried the bags into the kitchen.

"Do you think in Norwegian?" he asked as they put foam containers in the fridge.

"Usually. The longer I am here, the more I think in English."

"As in *wanna bet*?"

It was her turn to laugh. "As in. But you've seen me slip a few times."

"I hardly think of it as a slip. And it's charming."

She felt warmed by his choice of words. But all too soon, coffee in hand, they headed back to the office and the endless search.

"We haven't seen that man in a while," she remarked as she slid into her office chair.

"I wish that made me feel better."

She knew exactly what he meant. If the man were

an enemy, it was far better to have him in plain sight. If he were hiding, so much the worse.

AT SOME POINT, Trace began to mutter silently, then not so silently, at Allan. The thoughts he had weren't exactly nice, and occasionally they slipped past his lips as a quiet grumble.

Eventually Hillary, who was still moving through the stack of envelopes and sorting any other correspondence from Brigid, remarked, "Allan left you a mess."

"I'm wondering why the hell he didn't clarify this after Brigid was killed. Why hide it any longer? Unless he wanted to wait until he could report a full picture."

"I am wondering just how bad this will be when we piece it together."

Trace swiveled to look at her. "There's no need for you to take on this risk."

"I'm accustomed to risks. They don't frighten me."

Of course not, Trace thought. God, he wanted them both out of this mess, but he didn't want to betray Allan and Brigid. A lifetime of friendship was worth chancing a lot of danger.

Back to work building his own file of date-ordered emails. He couldn't escape that a warning must be hidden in this hodgepodge mess. Allan wouldn't have done this without reason.

Eavesdropping? Did he think the government might have been looking at his and Brigid's emails? If so, this mess was colossal.

But clearly Allan had been worried about something

bigger than an individual. No single man could access protected emails. The military was very careful about that.

Which brought him around to the NSA, but that seemed a whole lot bigger than would make sense, unless Brigid had stumbled on an extensive operation that could reach anywhere. Something that could rise to the highest corridors of power.

How likely was that?

How likely was it that two people would be killed over it?

His stomach began to turn sour. "I need to stop for a while."

Hillary looked at him. "Is something wrong?"

"Oh yeah. Two people dead. Just how big is this damn thing?"

She frowned. "I've been trying not to think about that."

"Maybe it's time we should both think about it. I don't care if my rapidly ending career terminates over this. But what about yours?"

THEY RETIRED TO the living room for some calisthenics. After that they repaired to the kitchen. Hillary hunted around to find a way to make hot chocolate. She found no cocoa powder, only an instant mix similar to what she sometimes encountered in field rations.

It would have to do. Besides, she knew how to make it richer—two packets to a cup and some of the heavy cream she had bought for cooking.

She washed the insulated mugs, used a handy electric kettle to heat the water and, when it was ready, she added a couple of spoonfuls of cream. The measurements were different from the metric ones she was accustomed to, but eyeballing worked just as well for this. She placed a mug in front of Trace, who seemed to be contemplating something over a far horizon, then sat with him.

Presently he said, "We may be looking at an octopus with a lot of high-level tentacles."

She nodded, having nothing to add.

"This should have occurred to me sooner in more than a passing way."

"Why? It's unthinkable."

"Until now, evidently. God, Hillary, we may be stepping into quicksand, and I don't want to take you down with me."

"There is always a way out of quicksand."

He shook his head. "You know what I mean." He shook his head once more. "I don't know why, but I was thinking of one bad guy. Or maybe two. I know we mentioned it, but I honestly didn't truly think beyond that to a chunk of upper-level command."

"Or a large independent contractor."

"Which wouldn't be much better. If it has important contacts within the military, then Brigid and Allan's cautious communications make sense."

She sipped her cocoa, hot and tasty enough to make up for the real ingredients. "Perhaps they didn't know but were merely being very cautious."

"Yeah, maybe. Until they both died." Now, at last, he sipped his own cocoa. "Not bad for a campfire quickie."

"It will do. I must say, Trace, that I find it just as appalling that a contractor might sell arms to the enemy. There is no excuse for whoever did this. None."

She stabbed her finger at the table, making a small thump. "A contractor stands to lose a lot, too. Huge contracts."

"Only if it gets out. Someone might cover for them. Everyone gets a few dollars in their pockets. The question is, how much money does it cost to get the right people to sell out?"

A question with no answer. Few of these questions had answers.

"Of course," he continued, "no military personnel need to be involved in reading their emails. Think about it. Who builds the equipment we depend on for secrecy?"

Ice ran down Hillary's spine. "Compromised communications?" There weren't enough curse words in Norwegian to express her feelings about that. Worse than arms sales. A threat to every single operation, every single soldier, out there. Out there anywhere in the world.

"You give me nightmares," she said.

"I'm going to have them, too. I'd suggest another run up the mountain, but look out the window."

She turned her head and saw snow blowing almost horizontally past the window.

Trace spoke. "And don't tell me you can do it. I know you can. But why risk a broken leg or a broken neck because we need to work off some stress?"

She didn't want to admit he had a point, but he did.

Some conditions should only be challenged for training or for combat. Being foolhardy was never excusable.

"You know what I'm going to do?" he asked several minutes later.

"What?"

"I'm going to take a few hours off. Nothing we can do now is going to bring Brigid or Allan back. So I'm going to declare it time to relax. I'll uncover the fireplace and build a fire. We can pretend we're out in some lost cabin in the middle of a blizzard."

She nearly laughed despite the serious fears they had just discussed. "It sounds like home."

"Even better then. A fire, a drink..." He trailed off for a few seconds. "You know, I think Brigid and Allan kept some brandy for special occasions. You like brandy?"

"Very much, for sipping."

"Hell, I wouldn't toss it off like a shot. What a waste."

There was a woodpile out back, and Hillary helped Trace carry in some logs and kindling. She left the building of the fire to him while she went to change into her thermal undergarment with a sweater over it and pulled on some socks. If they were going to be cozy, then she was going all the way.

When the fire started crackling and flames began to leap, Trace went to a cabinet on the far side of the living room and squatted, giving her a nice view of his backside in stretched denim. "I knew it," he said shortly. "But it's brandy and Bénédictine, if that's okay."

"More than okay. I prefer it."

He also discovered some snifters and after wiping

them out, he offered her a drink. She sipped with approval as she curled up on one end of the sofa.

"You don't mind taking some time off?" he asked as he settled into the recliner.

"I believe we have both earned it." Very much so. "I think your phrase is 'beating our heads on a wall.'"

A snort escaped him. "Just slightly." He stirred in his chair. "I feel like I'm desecrating space. This used to be Brigid's chair."

She pointed to the end of the sofa. "Then sit here."

"It's a stupid feeling."

"No. It's not. Now move."

He half smiled. "Orders again?"

"If they're needed." She sipped more liqueur. "This is quite pleasant with the fire."

At last he moved, sitting on the other end of the sofa. He lifted the brandy snifter to his lips. "You know the story of B and B?"

"I never looked."

"It's amusing in a way. A liqueur maker claimed he'd found the recipe in a destroyed Benedictine Abbey, then added the letters DOM for *Deo Optimo Maximo*, or 'God is great.' I guess it worked."

Hillary smiled. "The results hardly need the letters."

"Not anymore."

Quiet ensued, filled only by the crackling of the fire. Firelight danced over the wall, counterpointed by shadows. Slowly a realization began to creep through Hillary. She was feeling lonely. Lonely in a way she hadn't felt since leaving home for the army.

She guessed she needed her friends, her organization. Those who would understand and share with her. People she knew from the years behind her.

Trace was new, too new to reach that level of understanding, although he was slowly getting there when they talked.

She realized something else, too. It had been a long time since she'd had her arms around a man, or a man's arms around her. Her entire body had begun to ache for that intimacy, for the mindless pleasure sex could bring. She had been missing it for too long.

She had seen the reflection of desire in Trace's gaze from time to time, and Hillary was not one to hesitate once she had defined a need.

She set aside her snifter and scooted down the couch until she leaned against Trace. Hot, warm, hard. Their eyes met, his appearing surprised.

"Do you mind?" she asked.

"Hell no." He followed the declaration by putting his arm around her shoulders. "Get comfortable."

She did precisely that, leaning into him, resting her head on his shoulder. Male aromas reached her, enticing her further.

But she let it rest for the moment. Let matters follow their own pace. Take care she didn't intrude too far. Didn't demand what he might not be willing to give. Attraction was one thing. Following through was another.

He twisted a bit, drawing her into a more comfortable embrace. Her head slid down from his shoulder to his chest. His steady heartbeat filled her ear. She let her arm find its way around his narrow, hard waist.

The fire continued to burn, throwing orange light

around the room, promising heat. Her heart sped up a bit, and her body began to ache all over with hunger. She wanted more from Trace than this exhausting, probably hopeless quest.

He had so much to offer, despite his nearly compulsive drive to save Allan's reputation. To end his own doubts. She had caught glimpses of the man behind the immediate problem, and she liked him. She wished she could know him even better.

"Hills?" he said, unwittingly shortening her name to the nickname many of her friends used.

"Hmm?"

"Is this what I think it is? Or do you just want comfort?"

She turned her head a bit as he looked down at her and met his gaze. "Comfort, of course. But this is exactly what you think it is."

"Well, hot damn," he said.

"I don't understand."

"You will," he promised.

Then, before she could draw another breath, he twisted more and kissed her on her lips. Her immediate response startled her. Warmth became a blaze hotter than the fire nearby. Until that moment she hadn't realized just how much she'd been longing for this. For Trace.

His arm tightened around her shoulders. She tightened her hold on his waist. He tasted of brandy, but she did, too, and as their tongues dueled, it became the last bit of the old reality and gave way to a whole new world.

He whispered her name, then pulled her sweater

away from her throat, kissing and lightly licking her neck just below the ear. A delicious shiver ran through her, and her impatience grew as quickly as the heat.

She didn't want slow. She didn't want the teasing and tormenting. She wanted rough and ready and swift, an answer to hungers that were threatening to rip her apart with need.

She sat up, pulling her sweater over her head. "These thermals might be good for cold, but they're a nuisance now."

A laugh escaped him. "Sometimes all clothes are a nuisance."

TRACE WAS CHARMED. Enchanted. Never had he met a woman so bold, so immediately honest about her desire. Decisive.

No playing around with her, at least not this time. He joined her in pulling off their clothes as fast as they could. Hands and fingers tangled at times, drawing breathless laughs from them.

Then at last they were naked in the glow of firelight, but before he had time to really appreciate her beauty, she straddled him and claimed him.

Ah yes, he could get used to this. It was his last coherent thought as the pressure of need drove them hard, pushing them upward until they reached the peak together.

The explosion that ripped through him left him drained.

Hillary apparently felt the same way. She collapsed

on his chest, their bodies melting into one another. Neither of them moved for a long time.

HILLARY STARTED DRESSING, a chill reaching her despite the fire. Trace looked at her.

"You're wrapping up too fast," he said. "I want to admire you."

"Nothing unusual about me. You can look later if you still want to, but now I'm hungry."

He laughed. Hillary. She was unusual in every way. "You're a piece of work, Valkyrie."

She grinned. "I hope that is a good thing."

"Trust me, it's good."

He watched her stride toward the kitchen and enjoyed the view. Those thermals concealed very little, and she had a toned, fit body with long legs, just enough of a curve on her hips and rump.

And she was totally unselfconscious.

Smiling, he dragged on his own clothes, just well-worn jeans and a plaid flannel shirt that had probably seen its best days fifteen years ago. But that was the thing about his career. Civilian clothes lasted damn near forever.

He discovered her scooping their leftovers onto plates and warming them in the microwave.

"Microwaves," she announced, "are transnational, unlike measuring spoons."

He hadn't thought of that. He used metric measurements all the time on duty, but in a kitchen? "Maybe we should get you a set."

She glanced wryly over her shoulder. "I will not be doing that much cooking."

"I should bake those brownies," he remarked. "Chocolate would be the perfect topper right now."

After they had eaten the remains of the leftovers, Trace took over. The only hindrance was finding his way around the unfamiliar kitchen. At last he discovered the measuring cup and held it up to her.

"Look at that, Hills. Both English and metric measurements."

"It must be an error."

God, he was feeling good. He couldn't remember the last time he'd felt this good. There was something to be said for a decisive Valkyrie.

He did manage to follow the admittedly simple directions and get all the batter into a glass baking dish. When he put it in the oven, Hillary took over the washing up. He caught her licking some batter off her finger.

"Tsk, Hillary. Raw egg."

She flashed a smile. "I think I'm immune to anything that goes in my mouth."

She might be right, given where they'd been. "Well, the batter is almost always the best part."

"When I was a young child, I would beg to lick the spoon. I believe many children do that."

"I would have if we'd ever made brownies."

Her expression saddened. "Your childhood must have been difficult."

He shrugged. "I didn't think so at the time. I just built my life differently. But I told you that."

"Children adapt well."

Too well, he thought, as images came to mind, images he preferred not to recall. Lives he could not change.

They sat over coffee while the mouthwatering aroma of brownies filled the kitchen. He wanted to reach out to her, to at least hold her hand, but he didn't yet know where the lines were. Maybe she was done now. She'd satisfied her urge and needed no more from him.

He didn't want to be the creep a woman couldn't shake off.

He also didn't want her to shake him off. That would come soon enough.

"What about your friends?" he asked as the thought occurred to him. "Do they know you're staying here?"

"I called my first night and said I might be staying with Brigid's family for a while."

Brigid's family. The description pleased him. "So you think I'm her family?"

"Brigid would think so, I'm sure. As would Allan. And…" she shrugged. "Brigid was my sister."

"Hold on now, this is getting incestuous."

She appeared startled, then laughed. "Don't be silly."

Damn, he loved the sound of her laugh. He needed to make her laugh more often.

"What did you think of England?" he asked.

"Well, like many places, it depends on where you are. My mother is very upper class. She speaks like the queen."

Now *he* laughed. "A very particular accent?"

"Very. Go away from the palace, and there are accents I still don't understand. But we have dialects in Norway as well. I would say Britain has many dialects."

The timer dinged, and Trace went to pull the brownies out of the oven. "Was there anything you liked about your visits there?"

"The old castles. Everyone likes those. But I was amazed to learn that the queen owns all the muted swans on open water. Every year a tally is taken."

"That's wild." He couldn't imagine it.

"Some things began so long ago, when only a few owned everything. At least the swans are protected."

"There is that."

TRACE WENT TO check on the fire. Hillary wondered if he would add more fuel or if this period of rest was over. He must be feeling the pressure to get back to their task. She was beginning to feel it as well.

She closed her eyes for a few seconds, enjoying the memory of her sex with Trace. Swift. Hot. So satisfying. How good it had felt when he held her. Upon occasion she liked to feel soft. Womanly. Those desires hadn't been scrubbed out of her.

She wanted more. A lot more. A chance to admire him, to explore him. A chance for him to explore her. Long, lazy, slow.

But not now. Clearly not now. They faced something so enormous that neither of them could let go, not unless they could find nothing useful at all. Then they would have no choice.

Her thoughts drifted back to that man who seemed to have been watching them. Probably nothing, but along the back of her neck, she felt a prickle of apprehension. A sense she had learned ages ago not to ignore.

But one man? After they had begun to wonder about the scope of what Brigid may have discovered? One man seemed like a small response that resulted in two killings. Were there more that they hadn't noticed yet?

Their respite was over. She felt it in her bones. Time to get back to it.

She thought of Brigid. Of the bright light that had been snuffed out. Of the fact that it may not have been an accident of war at all. Of Trace's conviction that Allan had not killed himself.

Her own growing conviction that the two deaths were linked.

Trace returned and went to the sink to wash his hands. "Time to get back to it?" he asked.

"Yes."

He pulled two small plates from the cupboard and put large squares of the brownies on them. "Coffee?"

"Of course. Need you ask?"

His smile reached only half-mast as he started another pot. "We'll take this into the office. I need to find some paper napkins or we'll get too sticky."

Hillary knew where they were, having seen them during her hunt for cooking utensils. She pulled out a drawer and helped herself to a few of them.

Minutes later, coffee and brownies in hand, they returned to the office. There had to be an answer of some kind in there. Even Brigid and Allan couldn't read each other's minds.

As they sat and bit into brownies, Trace spoke. "If

this is as ugly as it's beginning to appear, we might be next on the killer's list."

"It's possible." The idea didn't disturb her. She'd been in situations where dozens of people had wanted to kill her. She wanted to live, but she didn't fear death. It often came swiftly and easily. She feared only surviving such an attack with her life in ruins.

"However," she said as she finished her brownie and wiped her hands thoroughly, "I cannot imagine that anyone is watching Allan's computer. Can you?"

Trace paused, then reached around and pulled a cable. "Not now for sure."

She shook her head slightly, then smiled. "If we'd found anything yet, that might matter."

"If we *do* find something, it *won't* matter."

No, it wouldn't. Not now. But the idea that someone might be monitoring Allan's computer didn't seem far-fetched. Not if someone had monitored communications when Brigid had been overseas.

Or maybe they were just turning into conspiracy theorists. That was possible, too.

STAN WITHERSPOON WATCHED from outside again, ignoring the icy night, ignoring the whipping snow. His cheeks stung, and even his gloves couldn't keep his fingers warm. He shoved them into his jacket pockets.

What was going on in there? Through a crack in one of the curtains, firelight was visible. A love nest?

Maybe so. Maybe he was worrying over nothing. The two of them might just be involved in the early stages of a romance.

Entirely possible, given that woman's beauty. Given that she was probably one of the few people in this county who could run with Mullen.

Hell. Double hell.

He should leave now. No one here would find him, not after all this time.

But fear held him rooted. Fear that they *were* looking for something. Fear that they might find something.

Fear of what his boss would do if those two learned something and passed it along.

No, he couldn't leave. He didn't want to die. That hadn't been part of his bargain with the devil. But secrecy had been.

Secrecy. God, what a mess.

Chapter Eleven

Morning seemed to arrive too early, although a leaden darkness shrouded the land. The snow had lightened, but a look out the windows told a story from the night: it had been a heavy snow, drifting everywhere it could find a nook.

The sight pleased Hillary. The beginnings of winter always sheltered the world in a silence muffled in white.

Trace was annoyed. "I need a run. And I hope we have enough hanging around in this kitchen to make breakfast. Of course, I could always walk to Maude's. She'll make sure we're provisioned for a week."

Hillary stretched and yawned. "A walk would be nice. I'll go with you."

They dressed for the weather, locked up and set out. The air held that unique crisp smell of a first snowfall. Hillary had never found words to describe it, but she always liked it. Not only did the snow dampen sounds, but it dampened all the other odors of life as well.

Smoke drifted out of many chimneys. No one was about except an occasional patrol car with a plow on the front of it. Their own cars were under a blanket deep enough that only bits could be seen.

A perfect pure world. Right then, anyway.

Trace spoke. "We don't usually see this much snow, at least not this early."

"Climate chaos," she replied.

"Not climate change?"

She glanced at him, feeling a bit impish. "Look around you. This weather the world over is chaotic." She paused. "The glaciers on the mountaintops at home have begun to melt."

"That's a tragedy. One of our national parks, called Glacier, has no glaciers anymore."

"Sad. Very sad. Some days I try to imagine Norway being green year-round. The idea hurts."

"The gifts of life are fleeting."

"So it appears."

At Maude's they were chilled enough to order some hot food to eat before Maude filled bags for them. The diner was empty of all but a few hardy souls.

"I'd offer you lattes," Maude grumbled, "but the damn things would be ice by the time you get home. The food in the foam containers won't be much better. They're working on clearing the roads, but I don't know if it's worth digging out your cars yet. Where would you go? I hear the grocery has hardly any staff this morning. It's not like us."

Hillary looked up at her from over a hot bowl of oatmeal. "Not like you?"

Maude sniffed. "Snow doesn't shut us down. At least not usually."

"We also don't usually get this much of it," Trace remarked when Maude had gone back to her kitchen. "We're not exactly prepared for it."

"Everyone should have skis."

She was pleased when he laughed. She could tell the melancholy mood was overtaking him again.

"Have you no plows?" she asked. "I saw them on the front of two of your police vehicles."

"Oh, we have plows. Just probably not enough of them. As for the police, if there's trouble somewhere, they can't wait for a plow to get through."

She nodded. "I should have thought of that."

"You can't think of everything, Hills."

Once again her nickname. She liked that he had arrived at it all on his own.

"Especially," he added, "when our brains are fried. I believe I have most of the emails in order now."

"Then we should start reading in sequence."

"I think so."

The walk home felt less invigorating than when they had set out earlier. They each carried three bags of food from a generous Maude, enough to get them through a couple of days now that they weren't running.

For the first time, Hillary felt uneasy entering the house. She turned briefly while Trace unlocked the door and caught sight of something moving. Something dark. Then it was gone.

Not until they were inside did she speak. "I saw something or someone move in the bushes across the way."

Trace dropped the bags on the small lowboy in the short, narrow hall. "Footprints."

She had no difficulty following his thoughts because they were already hers. She set her bags beside his, and together they started out. They should have a clear trail to follow.

The footprints were there as expected. They were scuffed together and smashed down almost to slush.

"He has been here for a while," she said.

"Yup. Split up?"

It would double their chances of finding the man. She nodded and started down the road in the general direction of the trail of footprints. Every so often she glanced to her right to check that they hadn't switched direction toward a copse of trees.

Not yet. Her instincts took charge, and when at last the footprints took a sharp turn, she followed them into the snow. Trace wasn't far behind. Then she reached the truck stop parking lot, already mush and ice from the heavy trucks beating it up.

She signaled Trace to swing to the left while she followed the outline of the parking lot to the right. Heavy trucks grumbled loudly, their engines and exhaust warming the air. And melting more snow.

No sign of footprints exiting the lot. Trace met her a minute or two later.

"Nothing," he said.

"Nothing," she agreed.

As one they turned to look into the truck stop diner.

"There is a crowd in there," she remarked. "No way to identify anyone."

"Nope."

"I only caught a glimpse," she told him. "It could have been anyone wearing a balaclava and dark jacket."

"That might well describe half the people in there."

"Any snow on him or his boots would have melted by now."

"Still not enough even if it hadn't. All those truckers. Many might still be dusted with snow, and their boots might be slushy from the parking lot."

Once more, Hillary walked around the lot in tightening circles, wondering if she could find any prints in the mess that appeared to follow a straight line from the ones they had been following. It looked like a stampede had run through that lot.

She hated to give up. Part of her training had involved tracking. She should have been able to find *something*. But not even the least little thing called her attention. Angered, she rejoined Trace, who had been doing the same thing.

"He knew where to run," she said.

He nodded. "Probably had it planned out in advance."

And they were, she realized, once again talking about the man, but now as if he posed a real threat. She imagined Trace wanted to get his hands on him. To shake him, perhaps, until the truth spilled out.

"Why," he asked as they walked home, "would the guy stay after he killed Allan? Hills, none of this is making sense."

"Only because we don't know the answers."

He snorted. "That's obvious."

She let a minor laugh escape even though she was

feeling deflated. "True. So is the fact that little of this makes sense."

"We have a ton of speculation, that's all. And if Allan didn't leave a clearer message for us, I may follow him all the way to heaven and give him a good shaking."

She glanced at him and saw that he was trying to joke. Good. She hated to think he might be close to despair.

Once inside they took care of all the high-calorie food Maude had sent with them. It hadn't grown as cold as Maude had anticipated, but it did fill the refrigerator.

"Back to work?" she asked when they finished.

"I want a few minutes first. I want to think about that guy."

"Speculate, you mean."

He grimaced. "Obviously."

Inevitably another pot of coffee. Inevitably another round at the kitchen table.

Hillary spoke while they waited for the coffee. "When my father and I are home together, we often gather at the table like this."

"From what I've seen, it's a popular place. Did you talk a lot?"

"Always. We played cards. Drank beer or aquavit. If it was an especially cold day and snowy outside, we gathered before a fire. Friends came over. I liked those days, but I mostly liked the private time with my father. There was never enough of it."

"Such good memories."

She eyed him. "Have you none?"

"A few." He didn't elaborate, though.

"How did you feel about your father disappearing?"

He cocked a brow. "Do you want the expected answer or the truth?"

"The truth."

"I was relieved."

That told Hillary as much as anything he had already said. She tried to imagine being relieved when your father left town. She couldn't. She had lived with the dread all her life that one day her father would never come back.

TRACE WATCHED EMOTIONS play over Hillary's face. A usually impassive woman, she was letting her inner life show. At least to him. A sign of trust?

But the man. Always the man. He kept popping up like a bad penny. Instinct told him the guy was definitely involved.

"What do you think of that man?" he asked her.

"He's around too much to be simply curious. He's also not very good at staying out of sight."

"I can't escape the question, though. If he killed Allan, why is he still here?"

She ruminated for a while. She poured coffee for them, then recovered a container of pastry from the counter. "Sweets. Sometimes I need them."

He nodded understanding.

"Okay," she said as she settled across from him. "Reasons a killer might stay in town. Because he's not sure the story ended with Allan?"

"Good one," Trace said. "You'd have thought the

results of the inquest would have been enough to send him on his way."

"Unless he fears there is some kind of evidence here."

He forked a piece of apple pie and drank some coffee before answering. "Then suddenly you show up and we spend a lot of time in the house. He might suspect what we're doing."

She made a face. "It's also possible he may think I'm your *kjære* come to visit."

"Kjære?"

He mangled the pronunciation a bit, but she didn't mind at all. She searched briefly for the English word. It wasn't one she had ever needed to use. "Sweetheart."

"Ah." He wiggled his eyebrows. "I should be so lucky. But that still doesn't explain why he's been hanging around for so long."

"No." She ate the rest of her pie, then got herself some fresh coffee. "All right. I agree, but this whole matter is strange. And if we are speculating..."

"Then anything is on the table. Could someone have told him about the emails?"

"You will make me shudder again. All the way to the top and beyond. So many lives at risk, so many operations no longer secret. I hate to think."

"If I believe that, then my anger over Allan's death will seem small in comparison."

"But we have to know for many reasons. All right, perhaps he has stayed because you made it so clear to everyone that you believe Allan was killed."

"Everyone in town appears to have heard about my meltdown."

"Oh yes, including the lovely Edith. I think even her dog knows."

"Oh for heaven's sake, Hills!"

The laugh shone from her eyes. "You made quite a spectacle, I gather."

He sighed and pushed his plate away. "I did," he admitted. "Nothing covert about what I believed. Bad soldiering."

"But good…" It was her turn to sigh. "I haven't the words for it. You are a good man. That's all it was."

"I was a little out of my mind at the time. Ignored. Helpless to make anyone consider anything besides suicide."

"From what Edith said, a lot of people believed you might be right."

"It would have been nice if they'd said so at the time. But what would have happened if they sided with me? An insurrection? Not likely."

She watched as he went to get himself more coffee. Nice view. Desire stirred again, but she pressed it down. "May I be bold?"

He looked at her, cup in hand, still beside the counter. "When have you ever been timid?"

"I can't remember. All right. We need to talk to your *sjef* of law enforcement. Your chief law enforcement officer."

"What good can he do?"

"He can hear what we suspect. Perhaps we might get some help with this strange man."

He looked out the window. "The snow has nearly stopped. Let me call him. Maybe he can spare some time."

TRACE CALLED THE department and asked to speak to the sheriff. Gage Dalton answered after a few moments, coming straight to the point in his gravelly voice. "What's up, Trace?"

Trace almost hated to speak the words, given the hard time he'd given Gage right after Allan's death. "It's about Allan."

"Oh?" At least Gage didn't sigh.

"We think we may have found something. And we think we have a problem. Got some time for us to walk over?"

"I have a better idea. I'll drive over. At least I'm outfitted with tire chains and a plow. Give me twenty."

When Trace disconnected, he faced Hillary. "He's coming over."

"Good. It will be nice to have a new wall to bounce the ball off."

He was charmed by her phrasing. Occasionally her English took unexpected turns. Sometimes contractions deserted her, and other times they slipped easily past her lips.

Gage was prompt. Trace caught sight of him limping up the walk through the window and almost winced for the man. Trace's injuries had been treatable. Gage's had not.

Trace decided he'd better not wait much longer to shovel the sidewalk. It was perilous out there, and while he hadn't expected anyone so he hadn't hurried to get to shoveling, clearly he'd been wrong.

He opened the door before Gage could even knock. "Sorry about the walk. I waited too long."

Gage gave his patented crooked smile, only one side of his mouth lifting. The other side of his face had been burned, and shiny scar tissue evidently deprived him of some facial mobility.

"Don't worry about it," Gage said. "You have no idea what I've tromped through already today. And my *own* walk isn't shoveled yet. Knowing my wife, she'll have it done before I get back."

Trace grinned. "She's in great shape."

Gage lifted a brow. "She's always been in great shape. Now she stays that way at the gym. Yoga! Anyway, she says she'll have to die eventually, but she doesn't have to get old along the way."

"I like that attitude."

"You would, being the guy who runs around this county like a mountain goat."

By then they were inside. Gage had knocked as much snow as he could from his boots and then hung his parka on a wall hook beside Trace's and Hillary's.

"Coffee?" Trace asked.

"You need to ask? Cars need gasoline. I need caffeine."

Trace made the introductions in the kitchen, and soon there was a cozy gathering around the table.

Gage looked at Hillary. "So you're Brigid's soldier friend."

"Yes."

"A wonderful soul, our Brigid." Then he turned his attention to Trace. "You said you had some stuff to discuss about Allan. I'm assuming it's not the ground you already covered."

"Not exactly. Let's start with the fact that Brigid was killed in late January. I know how that made Allan's death appear, even more than six months later. But consider."

Gage nodded. "Go ahead."

"Allan left me this house, but he also included all the passwords to his computer files in his will. I'd have come in here sooner to check it out, but…" Trace trailed off for a moment. "Gage, this place is full of memories for me, and, worse, it felt like an empty dark pit. I didn't *want* to come in here. And when I did, Hillary reminded me how strange it was that Allan left me all those passwords."

Gage sat up a little straighter, wincing as he did so. "It's strange, all right. My inclination would be to let things remain locked and hope the equipment got trashed."

"Exactly. I had to conclude that Allan wanted me to find something."

"I can see that. So you started reading."

"I wish. I found all the computer files scrambled. No date sequence to all the emails. He'd scattered them in different folders with no organization whatsoever."

Gage now frowned. "That's odd. Do you think he was trying to bury something?"

"Yeah, I do. Then I found a sentence from him in one of his last emails. He told Brigid to let it go. To just let it go. That was one of Brigid's favorite sayings, and very unlike Allan's temperament. It felt like a warning."

"Maybe." Gage was clearly withholding judgment.

Hillary rose. "I want to show you something."

As she left the room, Gage looked at Trace. "She's British?"

"Half, she says."

"Nice accent. Kind of lilting."

Just like Gage not to miss a thing.

"She's a soldier, too?"

Trace hesitated. "Yeah, sort of."

"What? What am I missing?"

"She doesn't want anyone to know, but she's Norwegian special ops."

"I won't tell a soul. But damn! A Valkyrie?"

Trace nodded, but if anyone in this town needed to understand Hillary's background, he figured the sheriff was it.

Gage offered another of his crooked smiles. "Pity the man who gives her any trouble in a dark alley. I've heard a little about them. But she's right. She doesn't want to become the subject of constant attention. Or of the grapevine."

"That's not what she's here for."

"I take it she agrees with you?"

"Maybe not at first. Now yes."

"Interesting."

Hillary returned just then holding an envelope. "It took me a few minutes to find it." She sat at the table and pulled the pages of the letter out of it, smoothing them. "This," she said, pointing as she moved the paper close to Gage. "The underlined part."

"'Too many guns,'" he read aloud. Then read it again. "Underlined. Heavily." After a moment, he swore. "I guess I know what you're thinking."

"Probably," Trace answered.

Gage leaned back, wincing again. "Discovering illegal arms sales would be enough to get a lot of people killed. Damn it all." Gage looked at Hillary. "I used to work undercover for the Drug Enforcement Administration. I'm suspicious by nature. This makes me *very* suspicious."

"Us too," Trace said. "But we need to comb through everything for more information, or we're at a standstill."

Gage nodded and rubbed the back of his neck. "More coffee?" he asked.

But he didn't ask Hillary, a gesture Trace appreciated. He went to get the sheriff more coffee.

"I need to think on this," Gage said presently. "I guess it was too easy to believe suicide under the circumstances. Especially since I knew how much trouble Allan was having with PTSD. Veteran suicides are all too common. But now..." He shook his head. "You're in a fine kettle of fish, and I don't know how I can help."

Hillary spoke. "There's one thing. A man."

Gage looked between them. "As in?"

"It doesn't sound like much," Trace admitted. God, they were handing Gage an awfully slim bit of evidence.

"Instinct," Hillary said flatly. "Trust our instincts."

Gage studied her for a moment. "Damned if I don't. I spent too many years having to rely on instinct. Go."

So Trace went, explaining the times they had seen the guy, but most especially that morning and how he had disappeared at the truck stop.

Gage rubbed his chin. "All right. A strange man. Not unheard-of around here since the college arrived. But this morning? I'd say you're going on more than instinct. A casual observer wouldn't have hurried away then covered his tracks."

"Exactly."

Trace was relieved that Gage didn't deliver a raft of reasons why it could have been innocent. If there was one thing Trace knew for certain, it was that he had grown awfully tired of being dismissed. He'd had an instinct about Allan. Now he had an instinct about this. By God, someone *had* to listen, and now Gage was.

Gage spoke. "You don't have a good description?"

Hillary answered, "If you suspect someone is watching you, do you stare back?"

Gage gave a short laugh. "Only in a restaurant." He sighed and took a swig of his coffee. "Okay, then. A stranger in dark clothes is showing an inordinate interest in you. When you show interest in him, he vanishes. That's a problem."

"And that's why I called you. I know you think Allan committed suicide, but—"

Gage lifted a hand, stopping Trace. "Let's be fair and honest here, okay? There was no evidence at the time to suggest anything else. None. We sure as hell looked for it."

Trace felt Hillary's gaze on him. "I've been running amok."

Another chuckle escaped Gage. "No kidding. You were more than upset—you were maddened. It seemed like no one was listening to you. It would infuriate me, too. We heard you. *I* heard you. But without evidence, we had to go with what we knew for certain. Allan had PTSD. I don't know if you have any idea how bad it was. He'd been shot up and discharged. Then his wife was killed and he started drinking heavily. Isolated himself as completely as we would let him. I personally kept doing welfare checks because he and I had hit it off." He stared at Trace. "I gave a damn."

Trace lowered his head a moment. "I wish I could have been here longer."

"Seems like you were dealing with your own heavy-duty mess. Anyway, everything I knew? It looked like suicide. But yes, we tried to find proof otherwise. Now maybe you have it."

"Not really. Just some threads. I was acting like an ass, wasn't I?" Trace looked at Hillary. "I went berserk."

He was surprised to see her smile. "A human response. We all have them."

Gage added, "Don't apologize." He looked at his coffee cup.

Trace read the message and went to get him more. "You need an IV drip?"

Gage laughed. "Sometimes I think so." He drained his third cup. "All right. I'll have my deputies keep an eye out for a stranger who seems to be stalking you in some way." He cocked a brow. "Most of the time we don't get a very good description anyway, so looking for unusual activity works pretty well. In the meantime, you two keep reading what you've got. Maybe you'll tumble onto a better clue, but for right now, my suspicion agrees with yours."

He paused. "It just seems weird the guy would hang around so long. Unless there was more than one guy here to begin with. Can't tell yet."

A few minutes later he limped his way out the front door and back to his vehicle.

"What happened to him?" Hillary asked Trace.

"Sad story. When he was undercover for the DEA, he went home to see his family. Apparently his cover had been broken. From what I understand, there was a car bomb. Killed his wife and kids and left him a mess in more than one way."

Hillary said nothing as she absorbed the story. "My heart breaks for him," she said presently. "Bad enough for someone to try to kill him. Worse that they killed his entire family."

She turned and headed back to the office.

Trace followed. The search had to continue.

HILLARY HAD TAKEN an immediate liking to Gage Dalton. He seemed sensible to her and like a good man to trust. Given that he must have helped reach the verdict that Allan had died by suicide, it was surprising how ready he was to listen to Trace.

But it also said something that Trace had phoned him in the first place.

Trace was soon clicking away at files and folders

again, dragging emails into his single folder where they'd be easier to review by date. Hillary resumed her study of the written letters.

Brigid had written a surprising number of them, as if she believed regular mail might be safer from scrutiny than emails. Or as if she had just liked to write her thoughts on paper, making them more enduring. It was amazing, however, because email had been a large part of everyone's life for ages now.

A slight chuckle escaped her.

"What?" Trace asked.

"Oh, I was just thinking of a time when I needed to write an actual business letter and I kept wanting to insert those emojis."

He smiled, too. "I remember the feeling. As if every sentence needed them for punctuation."

She tapped the stack of letters. "Brigid wrote without emojis."

"That's interesting."

"Irrelevant." Hillary shrugged. "It just struck me how they are changing everyone's writing, and I noticed only because they weren't there."

"You're going to make me laugh."

"Is laughter so bad, even now?" Some of the darkest moments in life were the best ones for black humor. It could help make life tolerable, but civilians would probably be appalled by it. Regardless, her comment hadn't been morbid humor. If it made Trace laugh, he needn't feel awkward about it.

Just about the time they both began to yawn and stretch, Hillary found another item. Her heart thudded.

"Trace? She writes here that she has seen 'it' twice. She doesn't explain."

Trace leaned over and looked. "What's the date on that?"

Hillary did a swift mental calculation. "Three weeks before she died."

He swore and stood up, rolling his chair backward with his legs. "We're onto something."

He left the room, and after a minute she followed, only to find him in the refrigerator. He glanced at her.

"I've got to eat. My mind is getting fuzzy. You?"

Only then did she realize how many hours had passed. Her stomach announced them with a pang.

"Life is getting pretty boring in some ways," Trace said as they pulled containers out. "We run, we eat, we read. Man, you're here for the first time and I should be showing you around. Giving you something to look at besides the inside of that office."

"I don't expect it. We have a task."

He had just begun to open a container when he straightened. "I'm going to shovel the sidewalk, clean off the cars."

"Sounds good," she responded and joined him in dressing for the outdoors. "My body is going to calcify in that chair."

"It feels like it."

He looked at her as they stepped out into the frigid air. "I guess now we know how often people in love communicate."

She laughed. "All the time?"

"Seems like it."

Hillary threw herself into shoveling and sweeping

with evident relish. Trace felt much the same. An ordinary task but one that loosened muscles, stretched his body. No running yet, but this worked a very different group of muscles. He almost wished there was more sidewalk and driveway.

Beneath the snow, ice had formed. Trace took the shovels back to the garage and brought out a bag of salt. Hillary had begun sweeping the snow from the cars with a long brush.

"There's an old military joke," Trace said. "So old that everyone has probably heard it."

"What is it?"

"You see that ice scraper you're holding? Well, the story goes that some guy is retiring. One of his men asks, 'Where are you retiring to?' And the soldier holds up an ice scraper. He says, 'I'm going to head south and stop at every gas station and ask them what this scraper is. The first place I find that says they've never seen one, that's where I stop.'"

Hillary laughed. It sounded even prettier on the fresh, cold air. "I haven't heard that."

"Maybe because you don't have any place far enough south for it."

"It would be hard to completely escape snow."

As they returned inside, wet pavement began to emerge from beneath the last of the frozen snow. The shoveled snow lined it like a white necklace. Overhead the sky promised more.

STAN WITHERSPOON WAS feeling fairly proud of himself. Hurrying into that messy parking lot had left no trail, and he'd had the sense to hide himself in the men's room just in case the two soldiers had seen enough of him to identify him on sight. He'd been relieved they hadn't come inside.

But he wasn't completely proud of himself. He'd allowed himself to be seen in a manner that had aroused enough suspicion to bring them looking for him. When he'd dared look toward the Mannerly house, which he could glimpse from the parking lot, he'd seen a sheriff's vehicle. His heart had stuck in his throat.

Stupid.

Stupid or not, he was among truckers who were mostly strangers in these parts, even more so than he. So he ordered himself a large breakfast, unsure when he'd eat again. It wasn't as if he kept his student apartment well stocked. Pointless to spend money on food he might have to abandon.

But now he had another problem to solve, and as the routine duty of eating soothed him, it cleared some of the fear from his mind. But not all of it. His hand shook a little as he lifted his fork.

He should just leave. Seriously. He hadn't heard of any trouble heading his way from Afghanistan. No ringing cell phone to alert him to a problem.

He'd tied up the loose ends and just needed to move on before he did something else stupid.

He wasn't cut out for this. Not at all. Three years in the Army hadn't prepared him for this. Damn, he'd been a clerk, a paper pusher, an inventory specialist. He'd never gotten closer to a fight than that argument with his roommate, a discussion that had earned him a punch in the gut.

No, he wasn't cut out for violence. It was one of the reasons he hadn't reupped even though he had no civilian prospects.

But it had gotten him this moneymaking job. It astonished him to find out how much more contractors were paid than the soldiers. Then he'd been offered a whole lot more money for falsifying the type of records he'd once kept honestly.

A simple enough task. Shave the inventory from the contractor shipment numbers.

Later had come the part about pulling a select but limited number of weapons from the crates in the equipment compound. As an inventory specialist, he had full access. Easy to remove smaller numbers of weapons, place them in a predetermined place and let the insurgents pick them up. He hadn't even had to deal with the money they paid. He never did know who was getting the money. He just knew what came down the pipeline every time he succeeded in delivering. But he had known enough about the insurgents to arrange Brigid's death.

He liked the money, though. A whole lot. It made up for a miserable life. In a few years he'd be able to retire. Nothing fancy, but he wouldn't have to worry about finding a job for years to come.

Then that Brigid Mannerly. Twice. The second time had been enough to warn him she didn't feel easy with what she saw through the chain-link fence. She wasn't just walking post. He knew the sentry schedule around the compound. Knowing was part of his success.

It hadn't been difficult to find out who she was, pretending he found her attractive. Nothing dangerous had begun rolling down the pipeline, but he set about arranging her death anyway.

Then his boss had told him Brigid was married and would be heading home to a husband in Conard County. He'd never heard of the place, but he found out quickly enough. Brigid's killing might not have been enough. Then he didn't feel safe even when he finally heard she'd been blown to bits.

The fear returned. Married couples didn't keep secrets from one another, did they? His boss didn't seem to think so.

Now here he was, a murderer. Twice. And contemplating two more.

God, he hoped he didn't have to do it again. And two of them? How could he get rid of two of them at the same time? They never seemed to be apart for long. Not anymore. He should have acted the first few days after that woman had arrived. Then Mullen had gone home at night. Now…

Now they rarely separated for any appreciable time. Hell. Hell, hell, *hell.*

LITTLE MORE THAN a quarter mile away, refreshed by showers and lunch, Hillary and Trace dived in again. They were whittling away the most recent letters and emails, carefully reading every single word for hints.

"I don't like this," Hillary said later. "Not at all."

"The job?"

"No. Time for a fresh pot of coffee or I'll fall asleep."

"We've been working hard," he pointed out.

"Yes, but we're not finding the head of this nail."

Interesting phrasing. He wondered if it was something Norwegian or something she had come up with all on her own. He didn't ask. What was the point? He just liked listening to her.

She washed the pot before starting fresh coffee. Then she washed cups, which had been standing for a while.

"I should have washed up," he remarked.

She shrugged. "Does it matter? I noticed it and I dealt with it."

He was much the same himself. Training. Experience. This time he felt he'd fallen down on the job.

While the coffee brewed, he went to look out the kitchen window. Snow fell again, but gently this time. The kind of thing you wanted to see on Christmas Eve.

"Do you celebrate Halloween in Norway?"

"More so now than in the past. Movies brought your kind of celebration to us, but beyond a carved pumpkin and trick or treat, I believe you call it, we don't decorate much. We tend to prefer house parties the weekend before, possibly with costumes."

"Sounds very civilized."

She laughed. "It's a time of year we like horror movies. One of my favorites is called *Dead Snow*."

"That sounds shivery."

She grinned. "Suitably so. Zombies."

"Oh man, you've got them, too?"

"Some things become worldwide."

He turned fully from the window. "Did we export them to you?"

She shook her head slightly. "I don't know. The word seems to go back a very long way. Should we look it up?"

"And go back to a computer?" He pretended horror, drawing another laugh from her.

"There can't be much left to look through," he remarked, taking his coffee and remaining on his feet. Chairs had begun to look like an abomination to him.

"Reading back to front didn't help much. Maybe we need to go the other direction. Something was building, yes?"

"They both apparently knew something was going on. I wish they'd tell us."

She didn't sit, either, instead leaning back against the counter. "It is there. We've found three references. We must be overlooking something."

"Maybe it's encoded in invisible ink."

"That would fit." She poured her own coffee.

"If you were home in Norway right now, what would you be doing?" His curiosity was honest. How different might her life be?

"At this time of year in weather like this? Well, the days are getting shorter right now, much shorter than here. Much colder. Other than that, I don't think we're all that much different than the rest of Europe." Her expression turned wry. "We *are* a modern country."

"Never thought you weren't. Just curious about cultural differences."

"Maybe some. I don't know. I don't live here."

He laughed. "True. I'm just curious, is all."

"Anything to talk about to avoid going back to that

damn desk, hunting for—what is your expression? A needle in a haystack?"

"That's it, and that's what we're doing."

"I know." She sighed and refreshed her coffee. "I don't like being hunted by that man. I want to get to him and find out what he's doing."

The guy truly troubled Trace, too. The big question, apart from what Brigid and Allan might have discovered, was why that man had hung around so long if he was involved in either killing in any way. The lack of answers bugged him and goaded him.

As a man of action, he hated sitting on his hands. He believed Hillary felt the same.

"I don't like the feeling we're caught in a game of cat and mouse."

Her mouth twisted. "But we seem to be. Are there any weapons in this house?"

The question told him all he needed to know about her state of mind. "I think Allan had some long guns in a locker in the basement. Maybe some knives, too."

"Then we should prepare. If this man was involved in Allan's killing, possibly in Brigid's, he will stop at nothing."

No, he wouldn't. But it still didn't explain why he was here two months after Allan's death.

That question bugged him as much as anything. Did he think Allan had shared information with Trace? Or that Brigid had shared concerns with Hillary?

"He may think we already know what's going on. Maybe I shouldn't have let Gage park out front."

There were no answers, damn it. Still no answers.

"Brigid never shared any concern with you?"

"No. But perhaps she didn't want anyone else involved. Perhaps she feared exactly what happened."

Trace swore. "I was afraid you might say that. It's been running through my mind, too, especially given the secrecy she and Allan have displayed."

"It's awful to think," Hillary said sadly. "Horrible. For her to live with that fear…"

No answer to that, either.

AFTER A FEW more hours of reading Brigid's letters, Hillary stepped out on the front porch. The snow continued to fall, more heavily than earlier, but no wind whipped it around. A beautiful winter scene.

Reading Brigid's letters made her sense of loss more acute. Brigid's personality and her love for Allan shone through as brightly as an unwavering candle flame.

That flame had been snuffed out. Originally Hillary had accepted the loss as the wages of war. She couldn't do that anymore. A simmering anger burned inside her that not even the waning, snowy afternoon could wash away.

Her hands clenched into fists at her side, a repetitive gesture she had tried to quell. Occasionally it still took over, and this time she didn't try to stop it. An expression of powerful inner turmoil, the need to punch something was strong.

Staring at the snow, she wished she had put on her skis. A good long cross-country would do her good right now, washing her brain with fresh cold air, working her body until it relaxed.

She didn't think it would be wise to run right now, although the temptation nearly overwhelmed her. But a fresh layer of snow could hide an underlying layer of ice, and it would help no one if a misstep sent her to the hospital.

It certainly wouldn't help Brigid.

At last her hands stopped clenching. Her nose and cheeks were beginning to hurt from the cold. Damn, she wished again for that balaclava. But she hadn't expected to be here this long. Summery clothes awaited her in an airport locker. From the Mediterranean coast she'd expected to return to Afghanistan. Cold-weather military gear waited for her there.

One corner of her mouth lifted. Living out of what amounted to two or three locations. Packing light, traveling often. A wanderer who had a firm home base.

Difficult as this visit had become, one good thing had come out of it: Trace. She was glad to have met him. Glad to have had sex with him. Hoped for more before she departed.

There was a meeting of minds between them. A mostly comfortable meeting. She hadn't wanted to grow close, but she had. Oh well.

Calisthenics, she decided. The only alternative to reach physical fatigue.

The image of herself, the Norwegian soldier, headed inside without challenging the elements of snow and ice, amused her. Her friends in her unit would probably laugh at her.

Necessary risks were one thing, stupidity another.

Chapter Twelve

They must have learned something. The thought gnawed away at Stan Witherspoon's mind like a rat. Why else would the sheriff have come over? Why?

He could think of no other reason, although he tried. He began to wonder if he should get in touch with the boss and tell him about this mess.

Surely the man hadn't held Stan responsible for that woman happening to walk by at exactly the wrong time. She hadn't been expected. Not a sentry that he planned for.

But the thought of telling the boss about this made him quail. He'd probably meet the same fate as Brigid Mannerly. Besides, the boss had told him to sew it up.

With two more murders.

Stan couldn't understand why he was balking now. He'd already caused the deaths of two people. Why not two more? In for a penny, as the saying went.

Except that he still recoiled from the idea. He hadn't figured out a way to pull it off, either. All his scrambling thoughts just kept pushing out more fear. And an increasing amount of self-loathing.

Possibly worst of all was that he'd begun to fear himself as much as he feared his boss. Yes, he had to save his own skin, but the price was getting too high for a man who'd been hired merely to fudge inventory and move some weapons to the perimeter.

Much too high.

The money was certainly less of a motivator than it had been at the outset. Money would do him no good dead or in prison.

Why hadn't he thought of that before?

Fear had driven Stan to the first awful act. Then to the second.

And now to two more. He was in this up to his neck with no way out.

He had believed himself to be a smart man. Now he believed he was a damn fool.

And a murderer.

"I THINK I found something," Trace announced.

With wind blowing snow outside, the office in semi-darkness, Hillary pivoted. "Where?" she asked.

"In the pictures file, if you can believe it."

She scooted over to peer over his shoulder. She saw what appeared to be a photograph of a page from one of Brigid's letters.

"Middle paragraph," he said. "I guess Allan destroyed the original."

I know what I saw, Allan. The first time I just thought it was a contractor employee checking out a crate. It bothered me in some way, so I walked by a few nights later. He was pulling out weapons and placing them on a tarp.

"Just what we thought," Hillary murmured.

"No accusation, though."

"She was too smart for that. I don't have to tell you. Her suspicion is clear or she never would have mentioned it."

He nodded and leaned back in his chair. "And the fact that Allan photographed the page means he felt the same."

"Which explains why I haven't seen the original."

"Probably." Allan drummed his fingers on the desk, then closed the file. "For now I need to stretch, to give myself some more heartburn with coffee and maybe eat something. Do you have any idea how many picture files that man has? I swear, he's got photos going all the way back to high school."

Hillary rose and stretched. "How did you find that one?"

"It was labeled *not for distribution*. I assumed it was some kind of sexy photo I would wish I'd never seen."

She had to smile. "Chicken. Have you ever watched a movie?"

"Yeah, but my friends weren't starring."

That at least pulled a laugh from her. He followed her out of the office, then watched her go to the living room, where she worked on stretching every muscle in her body. *Not a bad idea*, he thought. He was beginning to stiffen. But the damn coffee first. Once he had it going, he joined her in stretching.

"I don't think my neck or backside will ever be the same again."

She appeared amused. "Maybe not."

He uncovered the brownies to serve with the coffee, but neither of them wanted to sit at the table. A tradition broken.

Instead they stood holding small plates of brownies and sipping from mugs that wound up on the counter or perched on the table.

There really didn't seem to be much to say. They'd proved their suspicion but still had nowhere to take it.

"This may be a fruitless exercise," Trace remarked. "Brigid may never have shared any specific details about which contractor she suspected. She might have continued to be vague."

Hillary arched a brow. "Are we giving up?"

"Hell no. I don't think Allan would have been so secretive if there wasn't something more in there."

She nodded. "That's my feeling."

She put her plate down beside her coffee on the counter and began pacing in the small space. "I don't know about your training, but I was trained to put small pieces together so I would know what other questions might need to be asked. I am seeing many questions, but no one to ask." She spread her hands ruefully. "Like being a detective, I suppose. Maybe worse, because we can't just run around asking these questions of everyone we might know."

"That would be like allowing someone to draw a bead on us."

"Precisely."

He finished his own brownie and went to the sink to wash his hands and wipe a damp paper towel across his face. "Part of me wants to keep pushing, after finding that photo. Another part of me is in serious need of a break in front of the fire. Your options?"

"The break. We need to stay fresh."

But something in the twinkle in her eye suggested she had more than a log fire in mind.

Well, so did he.

ONCE THE FIRE was dancing on the hearth, they curled up together at one end of the couch. Trace wrapped his arm around her shoulders, and she leaned into him, her arm around his waist, her head nestled on his shoulder. He leaned back in the bend between the sofa back and arm, and she tucked her legs up beneath her.

That tickled him. This woman who had seemed as firm and tough as anyone in her job had become soft. Melting. She trusted him.

He savored the connection and wanted to take time to enjoy the feeling. No rush. These moments seemed cast in amber.

Eventually, however, the heat in his body rose to the level of the flames in the fireplace. Taking care to be gentle, he touched her chin with his finger and turned her face up to his.

A lazy smile resided on her lips. Her eyes appeared drowsy.

Bending, he kissed her, his tongue finding its way past her teeth. He felt a quivering response that drew him deeper, the two of them dueling slowly, exploring each other with tongues.

Hell, he was ready to run rampant. He had to remind himself to move slowly. There was so much he wanted to do, such as exploring her every hill and hollow.

Hillary indulged him for a while, allowing him to undress her then himself. When he sat again, he began his journey, kissing her throat, then kissing her firm breasts and nipples.

He felt her response run through her, felt her arm tighten around his waist. *Beautiful*, he thought. She was perfect.

He pulled a bit away to look at her from head to foot. Athletic, muscles formed by long hours of training but curves in all the right places. He ran his palms over her while he continued to suck her nipples.

Her quivers grew stronger. Her fingers traced his back and chest, heightening his desire. Oh man...

She finished waiting. With a sinuous move, she withdrew from him and lay back on the couch, parting her legs. He reached out to touch her between her legs, stroking silky petals, finding her swelling nub. This time a shudder ripped through her.

Then she startled him. "Trace, enough teasing." She held up her arms, and he wondered how any man could resist that invitation.

Moments later he filled her warmth and felt her wrap herself around him. A guy could get used to this.

Then the world went away.

Later they cuddled before the fire, still naked. The

time was precious. He already felt the ache of impending loss when she left. As of course she would.

But he realized he never wanted her to go away. A foolish, selfish desire.

Hillary then did a Hillary thing. She wiggled away from him and reached for her sweater and sweatpants. "It's time," she said.

"Time for what?"

Her smile was warm. "To move. To caffeinate. To eat something." She tilted her head. "You were right about this compulsion to eat. I never thought about it before."

Laughing, he rose, yearning for more of her but realizing she had other needs right now. Or maybe she sought some distance between them.

Much as he hated to think about it, he decided she was right. Their separate ways were far too separate.

He watched her prance from the room—really, it *was* a prance—and he grinned. She was a hell of a woman.

They ate slices of the whole pie Maude had given them. Warmed in the microwave, the apple pie was a perfect accompaniment to coffee.

"Tomorrow," Trace announced, "we're going to have to find our way to the grocery. Or Maude's. I know you don't like cooking."

"I don't hate it," Hillary answered. "It's just not something I'm inclined to do. When my father and I are home at the same time, we take turns cooking for each other. Then it is special."

"It would be."

She smiled. "Maybe it's special now, too."

Well, that pleased him. Not because he wanted her to cook, but that it might not be a pain right now.

While he washed up, Hillary disappeared. When she returned, she was garbed for outdoors.

"Going somewhere?" he asked, suddenly nervous for her.

"To walk around the outside of the house. It is snowing heavily again."

He understood instantly and reached for a towel to dry his hands. "Want me to come along?" He was sure she didn't, but he was uncomfortable anyway. Of course she wanted to go alone. If someone had been prowling outside, she didn't want to take a chance that they might reveal their awareness. More, if something happened, one of them had to be free to react.

Masculine protective urges surged in him, but he battered them down. She wouldn't appreciate them at all.

Hillary exited through the mudroom and out the back door. He couldn't hear a thing, but he didn't expect to.

Stealth was their middle name.

OUTSIDE, HILLARY STOOD on the snowy stoop, giving her eyes time to adjust to the night. Snow still fell heavily, but the wind didn't blow, so it wasn't filling in anywhere feet had stepped. It would cover the divots with a fresh powder, but the depressions would still be there.

She didn't believe that guy had given up when they followed him to the truck stop. If he was the man who had killed Allan, he should have left long ago. But someone had stayed and was concerned enough to watch her and Trace. No, he hadn't given up.

Same man? It didn't make a bit of difference to her. A stalker was a stalker. They might pose different kinds of threats, but given what had happened to Allan, she would have gambled that he was here for the same reason.

At home a night like this would have been an invitation to snap on her cross-country skis. This night she had other matters in mind—more important ones.

At last her eyes adapted. Her peripheral vision had sharpened, ready to notice any movement to her sides regardless of the nearly lightless world.

The night had turned shades of blue and gray. Only an occasional snowflake twinkled with rainbow colors as it happened to catch faraway light.

Now she scanned to both sides. Little light escaped from the house, thanks to those heavy curtains. Here darkness and snow ruled.

If someone had walked along the back of the house, she couldn't see it. Shadows weren't deep enough. The snow was brighter than the sky above, but not enough to overcome her night vision.

She listened intently. Sounds of distant people and cars reached her. Occasionally she thought she heard a twig crackle, but that was probably from the leafless trees at the back of the yard. At least, that's where it seemed to come from. Cold could cause branches to protest, and she seriously doubted anyone was up there in those gnarly fingers. Not a good hiding place right now.

On high alert, her every sense engaged, she stepped slowly off the stoop. She was well practiced at walking through snow without the noise of crunching or swishing. Slow, careful, light steps, following no rhythm. Minimal sound.

The world slept beneath its winter blanket.

She moved steadily, first to the left corner, then to the right. If someone had been trying to watch them, he must be disappointed. Not that he'd go away. No, he seemed too determined.

After she'd covered the entire back of the house without seeing anything untoward, she moved around the right corner. Watching before she moved. Attuned to anything else that moved or that looked too dark against the snow. Nothing.

But before too long, she saw the first depression in the snow. Right under the kitchen window. Her heart accelerated just a bit.

Then another and another. Instead of continuing, she retraced her steps and went around to the other side of the house. More dips in the snowfall. A short stride, probably because of the difficulty of moving through the snow.

A bigger hole beneath one of the bedroom windows.

She'd seen all she needed to. She headed back to the stoop and went inside. A bootjack by the door offered her an opportunity to kick the snow from her boots, then she entered the kitchen.

Trace was waiting for her with clear impatience. "Well?"

"Someone's been trying to look in the windows. I stopped when I was sure."

He swore and looked past her for a few seconds. "He's becoming bolder."

"Or more desperate."

She began to strip off her outerwear, eager to get back to that fire with another cup of coffee. Or maybe some hot cider. Creature comforts. She took them when she could.

"Trace? We are not chasing shadows."

"Clearly we're not. If we could draw this guy out, maybe we'd learn the whole story."

Hillary shook her head a bit. "If he's willing to kill to keep his secret, how much talking will he do?"

"Maybe he's keeping someone else's secret and will talk in an attempt to save his own hide."

After hanging up her outerwear, Hillary pulled out a saucepan and poured cider from the gallon jug that was stashed in the pantry. "You want some?"

"Yeah, please. I'm getting sick to death of coffee. I never thought I'd say that."

As the cider simmered, she added a cinnamon stick. "We like cider in Norway. Many different kinds with different infused flavors."

"Maybe someday I'll come visit and find out."

But his thoughts were elsewhere, she could tell. Nor did she expect his full attention. She suspected his mind was running in a direction similar to hers. The man knew he had been spotted. Now the question was just how much he was hurrying his plan. Or how dangerous that had made him.

She passed Trace a handled glass mug of cider, then ladled some for herself. "We need to be truly alert now."

"Yeah. Yeah. This is not a good sign."

They returned to the living room but didn't cuddle. Instead they both stared in silence at the fire. It was burning low, so Hillary added a log, then sat again.

Trace eventually spoke. "I don't like being in the middle of a mission without a plan. Not one bit."

She understood. "But what plan can we make? We don't know enough. Put booby traps around the house?"

He snorted. "And catch some kid out throwing snowballs. Right."

"You know I wasn't being serious."

She got his attention then. "I believe, Hills, that you have too much sense to even consider doing such a thing. My sarcasm failed."

She lifted one corner of her mouth in a half smile. "Not really."

"Okay, we've got to do more than read letters and emails. We may or may not find a decent clue there, but this man has become a looming threat. He could well be more dangerous than anything we might learn."

Hillary sipped her cider, grateful for the tangy warmth. "So come up with a plan, *Herre* Airborne. I agree with you, but we need to find a way to do it."

TRACE HAD TO LAUGH. In the midst of a serious discussion, she still managed to make him laugh.

Or maybe he was walking on air. Or in free fall.

Just then he didn't care. He figured he was going to care a whole lot before long, but right now he was determined to enjoy this time with her.

He sat back with his cider, liking every moment they

shared, especially the lighter ones. There was another side to the Valkyrie. One who was steadily creeping into his heart.

Man, he'd never expected this. There had been women in his life before, but none who stuck around and some he wouldn't stick around for. Nothing long-term.

This wouldn't be long-term, either. He thought of asking her how long she intended to stay, then backed away. The separation would come soon enough. Too soon.

"What about you?" he asked. "Do you have a plan?"

"Nothing beyond putting a man in jail. I suppose if he's watching us this closely, that we ought to be able to catch him."

"But how?" There was the crux.

"I wish I knew. Maybe your sheriff will find him."

"I'm not holding my breath. We're on our own, Hillary. I've been there before, and I'm sure you have, too."

She nodded. "Too often. When I'm interfacing with women, trying to learn something, I'm almost always alone. I don't want to seem like a threat."

"You certainly wouldn't learn much if you did."

She agreed with a slight nod of her head. "I suggest that after this cider, we go back to work. Maybe out of that will come some plan."

Trace doubted it. They'd already reviewed most of the stuff they had and had come up nearly empty-handed. Still, there was little else to do on a cold, dark night.

Well, there was something else to do, but he didn't

want to push it. He also didn't want to start feeling guilty about his desires replacing their true mission.

"Want to break it up?" he asked. "I'll take a couple of hours while you nap, and then we can switch."

Now she gave a clear shake of her head. "I trust you about many things, Trace. But not about waking me up."

"Caught," he admitted. "Then let's get to it."

HILLARY WAS STILL past knowing how late or early it was. Between her initial time change and the hours they had been working, unless they went out for a run, she had no instinctive sense of the time of day.

No running tonight, that was for certain. Maybe when the morning came, whenever that might be, the roads wouldn't look so bad. Well, except for that ATV trail they'd been running along. She doubted anyone would clear that except someone with Ski-Doos or the like.

In the meantime, there was the desk until they both fell asleep in their chairs.

IT WAS 4:00 A.M. by the clock on Trace's computer when he exclaimed, "Will you look at that!"

Hillary rolled her chair over immediately to peer over his shoulder. "Trace?" she breathed.

"Are you thinking what I'm thinking?"

Indeed she was.

They looked at a photo of a smiling Brigid in full combat gear, her assault rifle held in both gloved hands across her body. A typical pose for a soldier to send home. Hillary's throat and heart ached.

But what caught Hillary's attention and apparently Trace's was the big sign behind her. It appeared to have been painted on plywood, supported by posts. It had faded and peeled a bit because of the harsh elements. Regardless, while Brigid's body blocked the logo behind her, the words above her were readable.

BRIGGS AND HOLMES

And just below that:

Defending Our Troops

Trace snorted. "*Who* does the defending?" he asked.

"My thought, too." Hillary rolled her chair back a foot or so. "Quite an unusual background for such a photo."

"Quite a loud message if you have any idea what's going on."

Hillary abruptly jumped up and hurried to the living room. The grief she had felt upon learning of Brigid's death crashed over her with renewed force. For days now she'd buttoned it down, shoving it beneath a heavy boulder in her heart, focusing on finding any information that would explain the loss of her friend.

But she could no longer bury it. *Brigid. Oh my God, Brigid.* Dutiful until the end. Fighting for right at great risk. Bearing a soldier's burden. Unwilling to look away even when her husband warned her. Trying to protect her fellow warriors unto her final breath.

Hot, heavy tears rolled down Hillary's cheeks as reality once again struck home like a punch in her mid-section. This hunt for truth, as important as it was, had partly been a distraction from anguish.

Now, as that torment filled her, she felt her knees weaken. There weren't enough tears for Brigid. Not enough of them in this entire universe. Each salty drop mirrored a drop of Brigid's blood.

She didn't hear Trace approach. Only knew that he was there when his arms wrapped around her from behind and she felt his warm breath on her neck.

"Hills," he murmured, then turned her around, urging her to lean into him. His powerful arms held her, caring for her, and she took advantage of his strength, letting him hold her as sorrow ripped through her in successive, agonizing tidal waves.

"Hills," he murmured again, pressing his large hand to the back of her head, holding her even closer.

He let the pain rack her, didn't offer soothing words that wouldn't have helped at all. It seemed forever before she began to calm.

"I don't weep," she said hoarsely, her voice breaking. A few shudders still passed through her. "I don't."

"Of course not. This is all rain. I need to check the roof."

That pulled a watery half laugh from her. "I apologize."

"For what? For human feelings? Crap, even Valkyries can be human. You're not a goddess. Well, except when I look at you."

It was the right tone to take, and she rubbed her cheek lightly against his shoulder. "Do you know what the original Valkyries are? They choose who lives and dies in battle."

"Sounds like a description of a soldier."

She sighed, then pulled gently back. "Brigid," she said. "That photo. Brave."

"Brigid was always a damn-the-torpedoes kind of woman when she believed in something. That was the thing. She might tell us to leave it, to decide if it was important enough to waste our time on, but when it came to a cause, nothing could stop her."

"Not even Allan, it seems."

"Not even Allan," he agreed.

Hillary wiped her face with the sleeve of her sweater, then gave in to a need for comfort. She leaned against Trace once again, leaning as she hadn't in her entire adult life. She had sought comfort from her father in her earlier life, but never since joining the Army. She had friendships, but no more.

Except Brigid. With her, Hillary had found a relationship that extended beyond friendship. She might never understand why she and Brigid had been drawn together, or why they had become so tightly knit so fast. It just was.

It had been such a good friendship, too. Probably what Trace had felt for Allan. Maybe for Brigid, too. And of their losses, Trace had suffered the greatest: two friends he had known his entire life. She couldn't imagine the gaping hole their absence had left in him. It was too much to conceive.

Yet here in the midst of his own suffering, he was offering her comfort. A remarkable man.

"Coffee or sleep?" he asked. "Or maybe a drink?"

"Drink," she decided, reluctantly moving back from his warmth and strength.

She chose a beer, not wanting anything stronger. He joined her, popping the tops on two bottles.

Though she was hardly ready to think about it, she asked, "What should we do about that sign?"

"It's not enough to build a case, but it sure gives us a direction."

Hillary closed her eyes briefly, summoning the photo to mind. "A huge clue," she said presently.

"But only a guide. I would say, however, that we have the right idea about what was going on."

"What's still going on." Hillary felt more anger burn in the pit of her stomach. "Brigid started this. We've got to finish it."

MAYBE WE SHOULD check out Briggs and Holmes," Trace suggested. It was the only thing he could think of with what little they knew.

"We'll only find their public face," Hillary pointed out.

"Probably. But we might also find job listings that would tell us the kind of people they want to hire. We might even find some news stories that will tell us more."

Hillary raised her brows. "I think this company would want to stay very much below the surface."

"Or maybe they issue public statements. They must have stockholders. We ought to be able to discover what they were *supposed* to be doing over there."

She nodded slowly. "We might find some discrepancies. But we still don't know how to tie them to all this."

"Then let's damn well look for a way." He regretted the sharpness of his tone as soon as the words escaped him, but Hillary didn't appear troubled by it.

"We have to," she agreed finally. "It's all we have."

TWO BLOCKS AWAY in a nearly empty apartment building built for better times, Stan Witherspoon prepared for another day of stalking without being noticed. He suspected it would be harder than ever now that the sheriff had been called. Maybe there was a hunt for him even now.

He sort of doubted it. Those two couldn't possibly prove that the man they had followed had anything dubious in mind.

Besides, another fear had begun to grow in him. What if Brigid had said something that his boss feared enough to tell him to take care of it? What if it could all somehow be traced back to the contracting company he worked for?

Just because trouble hadn't fallen down the line to reach Stan didn't mean there was no trouble brewing.

Worse, what if Brigid had said something that would point directly to the contractor? Just a few words in passing that someone else had thought needed to be reported up the chain?

The thought made Stan shudder, and not from the cold. There could be an internal investigation right now, right as he sat on his butt trying to stay warm.

Stan didn't doubt in the least that his boss would have

a cover story that would point directly at Stan. Who, after all, had access to those crates? Who, after all, was capable of fudging the books?

He remembered all those times he'd sat around with other guys in uniform complaining about how much more contractor employees made than the stiffs in the service. Well, they had, and that had set Stan's sights on getting a job with one.

He'd never imagined that it would eventually extend to helping sell arms to insurgents. Not in his wildest dreams. But the money had been so great, he couldn't turn it down.

What if he'd stayed here too long? Yeah, he was required to return stateside for six months at a time, but that didn't mean nobody would notice the timing of his trip. Earlier than he'd been scheduled to take it. A claim of family problems.

That could be checked out readily enough if someone wanted to.

Stan swore every curse word he could think of and made up a few of his own.

He was a bean counter, for Pete's sake. Not a strategist. Not a planner. Not an assassin.

Sitting there in his darkened apartment, he wondered just how many potentially fatal mistakes he'd made.

The only way to save his skin was to get rid of those two people staying at the Mannerly house.

Except when he'd made his foray in the dark, he hadn't been able to see anything inside. How was he supposed to know where in the house they were, and whether they were sleeping?

He had no idea.

Nor was he a marksman who could kill them at a distance.

He had to separate them somehow. Get them one at a time.

He could do it. He just had to figure out how.

Chapter Thirteen

After a few hours of sleep curled up together on the queen-size bed, Hillary and Trace went back to work. Both of them were only slightly refreshed, but it was enough.

They ate the last of the leftovers in the fridge, which hardly qualified as a breakfast, then carried their inevitable coffee back into the office.

The first thing they reviewed was the photo of Brigid in front of the sign. Maybe there was another clue in it.

Trace enlarged it, and two pairs of eyes scoured it. Maybe that sign was the only clue Brigid had intended to send.

"If she'd sent more," Trace argued, "Allan would have figured it out. He wasn't stupid."

"What if he couldn't find out anything more to link this company to the arms?"

"I don't want to even think that. I want an answer to this mess."

Hillary sighed, rubbing her eyes. "So do I. I am just trying not to get my hopes too high."

"Hope? I'm beginning to wonder if I even know what that is. I'm just determined."

Hillary was, too, but she insisted on looking at the photo longer. She stared until she thought her eyes would turn into flaming coals from the intensity, but then she spied it.

"Trace."

He turned his head. "Yo."

"Look at the photo again."

"I've been staring at it for the last half hour."

"Just look." She pointed with a finger. "Shadows."

"Shadows?" But clued in now, he studied them closely. "There's something wrong."

"The light. The photo of her was taken at a different time of day than the photo of the sign. Look at the difference in the shadows. The time was far apart."

He leaned in, then murmured, "My God. My God."

"Tell me if you think I'm wrong, but the photo of the sign was taken under artificial light. As if some light source is shining on it."

"And Brigid appears to be photographed in the morning or the afternoon. You're right! She must have worked hard to layer the two pictures."

"And include the shadows," Hillary agreed.

"Damn, I wonder if I can take the layers apart."

"I don't know how. When she sent it, it was one photo." She picked up their cups. "I'm getting more coffee. And there must be something left in the cupboard."

"More brownie mix." But he sounded far away, as if lost in thought. Hillary's own brain was turning around, seeking some way to use this information.

Brownies? She could have laughed, then decided the chocolate and sugar might be helpful. She only wished she'd thought to buy a box of instant oatmeal, but at the time she'd believed she'd only be staying a few days.

She pulled the curtain back a bit to see the morning was clear and sunny. Maybe she should walk to Maude's and get them a meal.

Almost as soon as she had the thought, she discarded it. If Trace was going to be diving into that photo, she wanted to be here for it.

But just as she was about to put the wet ingredients into a mixing bowl, Trace appeared.

"I locked up the photo under a new password. Now we're going to get out of here to buy some decent food. We can't live on brownies and leftovers, and neither of us really feels like cooking. Even if you do have cod in the freezer."

"I agree." Getting out would feel so good. Sunlight. Chilly fresh air. Snow crunching under her boots. She was not built to stay inside for so long.

"Maybe it'll drive out the fog in our heads."

"I could use that."

The walk to Maude's was wonderful. Hillary felt her head clearing, the staleness that filled her lungs and brain blowing away. It was cold, but people were about, apparently glad to escape from the winter storm. Rosy faces smiled. Cheerful greetings rang out. Trace answered them all with a smile and a wave.

Hillary was happy to see his hometown taking him back into their embrace. It must have been hard for him to feel like an outsider ever since he'd refused to accept Allan's death as a suicide.

Brief as the walk was, Maude's felt hot inside. Between her kitchen and all the people who preferred to eat in their shirtsleeves rather than winter coats and jackets, she probably kept her thermostat high.

As Trace came to the counter, Maude eyed him.

"Let me guess," Maude said. "Food for half an army and all of it takeout."

Trace laughed. "Plus lots of veggies. Whatever you've got. We've been missing them."

"Stick your nose out once in a while and you won't be missing anything." Then she looked at Hillary. "Do I misremember, or do you like oatmeal?"

"Very much."

"Well, I've got a box for you to take back with you, if you know how to cook it."

Hillary smiled. "I think I can. Thank you."

Maude nodded. "Now you two go sit down while I get the food ready. Since I'm missing half my regular customers, it shouldn't take too long."

A few minutes later, a clone of Maude showed up bearing two tall insulated cups. "Hot lattes. My mother says you look like you're freezing."

Trace looked at Hillary. "Is my nose blue?"

She shook her head, a smile lurking around her lips. "I suspect mine's as red as yours, though."

They unzipped their jackets and enjoyed their coffee while they waited.

Hillary remarked, "You didn't ask for anything in particular except vegetables."

"That's because Maude will take care of us. Besides, everything on her menu is good. We might get a bit of most of it." He smiled. "Think of it as a treasure hunt."

About a half hour later they were heading back to the house with a whole bunch of plastic bags full of goodies.

"I can hardly wait to see what she gave us," Trace remarked. "Dang, that woman is softening with the years. I swear she used to be a fire-breathing dragon."

"Maybe she just likes you."

"Ha!" he answered. "Maude is famous for not liking anyone. Well, except Gage and the old sheriff. She must have a soft spot for cops."

"And maybe for soldiers, too."

Back at the house, they unpacked, peeking into the containers. No question but Maude had been generous and had given them a large variety of meals. As for veggies, there was a ton of broccoli, plenty of carrots and a few large chef's salads.

"Those salads won't last long," Hillary remarked.

"A good reason to start eating. That's ranch dressing on the side. Let me check what might be in the fridge."

He soon emerged with bottles of blue cheese dressing and creamy Caesar. "I hope one of these is to your taste."

"Blue cheese. In any form on almost anything."

Hillary left the box of oatmeal on the counter as a reminder to herself. She could eat it at any time of day.

They decided to dive into the salads immediately, along with the croutons Maude had packaged separately.

"Oh man," Hillary said. "Every cell in my body is happy."

Trace crunched on some lettuce, then agreed. "I think she included some sliced cheese, too. That woman thought of everything."

After cleaning up, they headed again for the office. Hillary paused. "I saw some pavement out there. The snow is melting."

"True." Trace flashed a smile. "We couldn't run all the way because I'm fairly certain a lot hasn't been plowed yet. Nothing out there but parks. Wanna go anyway?"

"Is that even a question? Calisthenics haven't been enough."

Twenty minutes later they were trotting along the road. *Such a beautiful day*, Hillary thought. Even the air felt a little warmer under the sun. As they fell into step together, she had the oddest feeling that she'd come home.

THEY WERE ONLY able to complete half their usual run, but they arrived back at the house feeling pleasantly relaxed anyway. A brief burst of freedom. Of self-care.

Hillary's mood had leavened considerably. The run had done her wonders, and Trace looked as if he felt the same. They'd been stapled to their chairs too much. Yes, it was important, but so was moving around, working muscles. The endorphins were pretty good, too.

After they ditched their winter clothes and boots, choosing to walk around in socks, they grabbed some coffee and headed to the office for another kind of marathon.

"I've been thinking about that photo a whole lot," Trace remarked as they marched down the short hallway and into the office.

But as soon as she crossed the threshold, Hillary froze. "Trace?"

"Yeah."

She pointed to the stack of letters that had been on her part of the desk. The pile was smaller, and many appeared to be gone.

Trace understood immediately. At once they both went on high alert and with hand signals agreed to take different parts of the house to find out if anyone was still there.

Hillary headed for the living room, a place full of many hiding spots, especially with the room darkened by the curtains.

Trace took the back of the house, where three bedrooms offered more hiding places. They moved slowly, silently, peering around corners before entering a room.

Hillary found nothing in the living room. Trace was taking longer in the bedrooms, so she went to check the mudroom.

There was no mistaking that the back door had been jimmied open.

She cursed under her breath, wishing she had her boots on so she could track outside. Well, she could get them now.

"Hillary?" Trace still spoke quietly as he came up behind her.

She pointed to the lock, then at her feet. Trace nodded and slipped away. Two minutes later he was back with both their boots and their insulated vests.

Outside the day was still crisp and fresh, dimming a bit as the afternoon deepened. Unmistakable boot prints covered the stoop and led away toward the trees. But there were also prints leading to one side of the house.

Again they split up, Trace heading for the trees, Hillary around the side of the house. Nothing but the footprints, the ones on the side of the house coming from the street, the ones at the back heading toward the trees.

Trace took off. Hillary waited in case he wanted backup of some kind. Not that he couldn't take care of just about anyone out there. But someone who was armed? Two people would do better. But the house still needed protecting. Much as she hated being the sentry, that was what was required just then. The invader might come back. Or if Trace called out, she needed to be ready and not already in trouble.

But the beautiful day, no longer as beautiful, remained silent.

At last Trace returned. He shook his head, and she waited for him to reach the stoop.

"A car," he said when they got inside. "A car. I'd call the sheriff, but it looks as if quite a few vehicles have been up and down that alley today, including the garbage truck."

"Apparently that man knows what we're doing, and he's getting desperate enough that he doesn't care if we know."

Trace's answer was harsh. "He won't be prepared for what he'll find in *this* house."

TRACE WAS ANGRY. Not a bit afraid or unnerved, but furious. Whoever had done this clearly knew something about what had happened to Allan and Brigid. There could be absolutely no other reason to break in here. Especially since nothing appeared to have been touched except Brigid's letters.

"God," he said. "That was a violation. Her privacy. His privacy. Even if they're gone now, no stranger has a right to invade their intimacy in such a way. No stranger has a right to invade their love."

Hillary nodded her agreement. She hadn't been any happier about reading through all those communications than he had been.

Trace attempted to lower his fury a few notches, but he didn't succeed. It wasn't just knowing that Allan, and possibly Brigid, had been murdered. No, it was the invasion. Matters they would have shared only with each other had now been stolen for some creep to read.

They returned to the office with bottles of beer, but Trace didn't face the computer. With his chair turned sideways, he looked toward Hillary but barely saw her. There was a blackness growing in him, a blackness he had felt only in the heat of battle. As if his soul were being scooped out, to leave a dark void behind. It wanted him to fall in. To never emerge again.

It was a hole he had felt only when the bullets were flying, when the bombs and grenades came his way. When death exploded the world and sometimes claimed his buddies. When all that was civilized was stripped away.

This creep was pulling him back there, to places in himself that he had never liked no matter how necessary. If that guy showed up right now, Trace would have throttled him with his bare hands.

"Hills?" he said, once again seeing her and not the pit inside him.

"Yes?"

"It would be murder if I kill that SOB."

She placed her bottle on the desk and leaned back in her own chair, studying him gravely. "Legally, it probably would be. I don't know your laws. Maybe if he comes inside this house when we're here, it wouldn't be. If he attacks, it wouldn't be."

"But there's always a set of conditions that protects *him*. Always."

"Rules of engagement."

The rules soldiers were supposed to follow. He sighed, rubbing his hands over his entire face. Trying to erase thoughts he didn't want to have. Rules of engagement. A guide that worked except in the heat of a battle.

"It can be a struggle," she remarked. "When we go to war, we are expected to be no longer civilized in many ways. When we come back, we are supposed to become civilized again."

"It can be a leap," he admitted. He looked to his blank computer screen again and realized he didn't want to dive back in. Not yet.

He turned his attention back to Hillary. "You have any PTSD?"

She shrugged. "I'm fortunate. It hasn't been disabling. You?"

"Yeah. I've been so wound up in this mess that it's been leaving me alone. I've been luckier than a lot of my buddies, though. A lot luckier."

But here he was, hovering on the brink of another pit

that could suck him in. One that he'd been successfully battling. He forced his attention away from the internal war to the external problem. "There's got to be more information in that photo than we noticed."

"I think so. It was certainly pointed."

"Yeah. Brigid always knew what she was doing." Swiveling around, he woke up the computer and unlocked the photo. It hadn't changed any, but he tried to see it with fresh eyes.

"Can you change the colors in the photo?" she asked.

"I'm no geek, but I can try. Why?"

"Steganography."

A few seconds passed before he recalled the word. "As in a hidden message?"

Hillary nodded. "Those conflicting shadows may not have been intended just to identify a contractor. We can try changing the colors first to find out if anything looks out of place. Then we could try examining it pixel by pixel."

He stared at the photo. "It wouldn't be beyond Brigid to figure out how. She was always good with technology. Now I wish I'd gotten a degree in computer science."

An amused sound escaped Hillary. "I doubt steganography is one of the classes. Try looking it up online. There might be some suggestions how to do this."

A few minutes later, he groaned. "Damn, Hillary, do you have any idea how many ways there are to do it?"

"I was afraid you might say that." She looked over his shoulder and sighed audibly, warm breath on his neck. His mind leaped immediately to other things they might be doing, but he reined himself in. Kept going on the problem.

He spoke. "It had to be something Allan would recognize, would know how to decode. Naturally he left us a packet of directions."

The sarcasm in his tone was audible, and he wondered just how irritated with Allan he was becoming. "Okay," he said. "I already need a break. Maybe moving around will get my brain back in gear."

She lingered a few minutes looking at the photograph, but soon joined him as he paced through the house, leaning her shoulder against a doorjamb and folding her arms as he passed by.

She spoke. "It has to be in the image. That removes quite a few methods."

"Sure. But that still leaves a lot of methods I don't know how to break through." He turned into the kitchen eventually and pulled out a container, inspecting the contents. Then he placed half a club sandwich on each of two plates. "Fuel up. We're about to take a long march."

This time he didn't reach for beer but instead started coffee. "God, I don't think I've ever drunk so much coffee."

"Neither have I. I'm starting to feel a bit of stomach burn."

"The food should help. If not, I'm sure there's some antacid in this house somewhere. What house would be without it, these times we live in?"

Another amused sound escaped her.

"What?" he asked irritably.

"You're actually charming when you're so frustrated."

"Charming?" Then he replayed his own words and tones in his mind. "Sorry."

"I'm not annoyed. I share your feelings. I just like the way you express them. Nothing held back."

Trace shook his head as he placed the plates on the table and dug out a couple of napkins. "Oh, I'm holding a lot back. I want to shake Brigid until her teeth rattle for not listening to Allan. I'm furious at him for not taking action with whatever information he had. He could at least have reported his suspicions."

Hillary grew so silent that he stared at her. "What?" he demanded finally.

Her words fell like bombs. "Perhaps he did."

HILLARY SUPPOSED THE sandwich was delicious, but it might as well have been sawdust for all she tasted it. She suspected that Trace wasn't feeling any differently. He ate mechanically, but he talked.

"If he reported it, something should have been done." Then he answered himself. "Unless he reported it to the wrong person."

"Possibly." She forced down another bite, then went to get a glass of water to help her swallow. The coffee remained untouched in its pot.

"Are you suggesting that Allan got killed because he told someone what he knew?"

"It's possible. I don't know. There must be layers to this arms sales business, but where are they? How deep is all this? How high does it go? I can't imagine he would have reported it to the contractor."

"That doesn't seem likely," Trace agreed. "What if we find a hidden message in that photo? Who do *we* report it to? How can we know it's not the wrong person?"

Hillary mulled it over for all of ten seconds. "I go to *my* chain of command."

"Are you saying Norwegians never get up to dirty business?"

"No. What I'm saying is that it's unlikely any of my countrymen would be involved in this *particular* dealing. Allan would have reported to someone he knows, most likely in your military. Not in mine."

She paused. "I am not claiming any moral superiority. We also have our own arms manufacturers and deals with foreign governments. Weapons merchants are everywhere. It's just that this situation, involving an American contractor, would be unlikely to extend to the Norwegian military or companies."

He nodded grimly. "Okay. If we find something useful, you take it up your chain of command. Then duck, because if this extends across the alliance, we're going to take a dangerous ride."

"I think neither of us has ever avoided danger."

He then said something he figured she wouldn't like because she was so strong. But it burst from his heart anyway. "I couldn't stand it if anything happened to you."

She didn't bristle, not even a bit. Her answer was simple. "Nor I to you." Then she returned to Valkyrie Hillary. "We have a mission."

Easier said than done.

Chapter Fourteen

Stan Witherspoon was becoming an inveterate pacer. When the walls of his tiny apartment with its bedroll on the floor and its miniature kitchen covered with empty food containers became too confining, when he wasn't trying to see what that damn Mullen was up to, he paced in the courtyard created by the four surrounding apartment buildings.

There was hardly ever a soul out there, but Stan had paced enough to flatten all the snow into a hard, icy path around the perimeter.

He was a damn fool. A bigger fool than he'd ever guessed, and he was quite sure that he'd never overestimated his own intelligence. He knew enough to get by. He knew enough to fudge an inventory.

But he'd dropped out of college when he realized he'd never pass the CPA exam no matter how hard he studied. His father had wanted him to join the firm, but Stan knew better. He knew he was better off disappointing his father at the outset rather than after a mediocre performance during four years of college to be followed by failing the CPA exam.

His dad had at least looked impressed when Stan had told him about joining the contracting firm and the kind of income he was making. But money had always mattered to the senior Witherspoon, a trait he had passed along to his son.

Well, his dad wouldn't be impressed now, and neither was Stan. He was in a bind so tight that it sometimes felt like his head would explode from the pressure.

He'd taken care of the Mannerly guy according to his orders. It should have ended there. He should have just left town. Instead he'd had to stay. Because of that Mullen guy. Because he was making such a ruckus about murder.

Because he might know something.

But even non-Einstein Stan Witherspoon knew he'd made a major mistake earlier. Even though he'd been noticed, he hadn't been noticed enough to get himself in trouble. He doubted the sheriff was looking for him. Cripes, he'd made himself as invisible as he could, as unremarkable-looking as he could.

But today. Today he'd made a gigantic mistake.

Walking around outside, he wanted to pull out his own hair. He wasn't a burglar. What made him think he could break into that place and have anyone think it was a random robbery?

He should have taken something valuable. Like the TV. Or the sound system. Or even the computer sitting on that desk surrounded by papers. Except that he'd known that carrying that stuff from the house might have drawn the kind of attention he was seeking to avoid.

No, all he'd taken was some of those letters. The most recent ones from Brigid Mannerly. Hoping to discover what Mullen knew, if anything. To find out what the Mannerly woman might have revealed to her husband. Hoping that those two people staying there wouldn't notice. Why should they be interested in a stack of letters? Why was he stuck in this town making messes everywhere he went?

Because somebody up the chain had plucked a string somewhere. Because someone had made his boss nervous.

The cold penetrated the fog in his brain, and he realized abruptly that he needed to get inside. Afghanistan wasn't a hot climate, but he was finding it bothersome to adapt anyway. Or maybe it was his own fault for spending so much time outside accomplishing very little.

Except getting himself closer to trouble. When he got inside, he didn't even want to take off his outerwear.

He was cold to the bone, and he knew it wasn't the weather outside. No, this was the iciness of terror.

Death was creeping closer, and right then he couldn't imagine a good way to hold it off.

TRACE THREW UP HIS HANDS. Hillary almost followed suit. Her eyes burned and felt as if they wanted to fall out of her head. They'd been manipulating that photo for hours and seemed to be getting nowhere near any kind of message.

"And there's nothing useful in her letters," Trace grumbled.

"Not that I found. Emails?"

"I can start running through them again. Maybe I should just print them all out so that you can look with me."

"I wish that man hadn't taken her letters." Hillary felt sorrow tug at her heart.

"Me too, but, joy of joys, I found a folder where Allan scanned them all. They're still here, Hills."

"But you haven't read through them again?"

"Who's had time?"

She shook her head and stood up, shaking her arms and rotating her shoulders. "I'm convinced there's a message hidden in that photo. We just need to find a key."

"That's like going into a store and asking them to make a key without giving them a template to use. I'd just like to find a note from Allan saying flat out that this is what we need to do."

She barely managed a wan smile. "Considering how secretive they were being…"

"Yeah." Trace stood with her. "Calisthenics?"

It sounded like the best idea in the world. Hillary went to her bedroom to pull on her loose-fitting sweatpants and a T-shirt. Laundry again tomorrow or she was going to smell like the inside of a goat shed.

Eyeing Trace as they worked out was probably the most pleasurable thing she'd done since their walk to Maude's. The walk stood out in her mind the way a sparkling ornament stood out on a Christmas tree. And now this.

She'd heard the term *eye candy* somewhere, but now she knew what it meant. When they finally finished and began walking around the room to cool down, she told him frankly, "I'd like to climb into bed with you."

He straightened from the twist he was doing. "Seriously?" His brows had lifted, and a grin started to spread across his face.

"Seriously." Then she unleashed a light laugh and dashed toward the door. "I take the first shower."

"Maybe not alone," he retorted.

Nor did she.

THE WATER WAS WARM. Trace's soapy hands running over Hillary from top to bottom made her burn hotter far more than the water. How Trace managed to lather her and bend over in the small stall was something of a miracle in itself. But he did, even reaching the arches of her feet. When he began to wash her center, heat exploded into a firebomb.

But first she wanted to give him the same treatment. She took the slippery bar of soap from him and acquainted herself with every hard muscle, front to back. When she heard a soft groan escape him, she smiled with pleasure.

Hard, firm, perfect in every line. Staring into his face brought her a different kind of pleasure. She just plain liked his face. The sight of it warmed her in a wholly different way. Handsome. But more than handsome. Despite his hard edges, he could soften, and she saw it now.

They came together in a slick embrace, their kiss tasting like soap.

"Damn," Trace muttered. "We'd better get out of here before we slip."

She hated the thought but had to agree. But next was toweling each other off, massaging skin with soft terry cloth. Desire began to rumble like thunder on the horizon.

Then the ringing of a phone came from another part of the house. They both stilled and stiffened.

"That's not my phone," Trace said.

Grabbing a towel, Hillary swiftly wrapped it around her head. "It's mine. It may be my father."

"Go," he said with a laugh. "Go. There'll be time later."

She hoped so. Unless their brains started whirling over the mystery again. It never stopped niggling at her, at least not for long. The shower interval had been one of those rare times. Trace swept her away from reality with such ease. With such wonderful touches, as if he knew her body as well as she did.

She reached her phone, which was sitting on the night table beside her bed. She hadn't expected to need it except for an emergency, and her heart galloped as she wondered if something had happened to her father.

"Hills," said his warm, deep voice in her ear. "Where have you gone? Your friends say you went to America and decided to stay for a while?"

"Well, I'm in America and I decided to stay, Pa. Are you all right?"

"As fit as I've ever been. Staying young by climbing mountains. The snow is getting deeper. How can you give up your time in the South of France? Or is it more beautiful there?"

"It's...different. But there are mountains. Even some snow, but I don't have my skis."

He laughed. "If you were here, we'd take a long ski and camp under our favorite trees."

"I miss you, Pa."

"I miss you, too. But I won't miss you for long, I hope. A desk has taken over my life."

"No." Surprise hit her.

"Yes. My time has come. Now I write orders for everyone else."

It was her turn to laugh. "That sounds comfortable."

"Too comfortable. But the mountains are still here to keep me busy. When will you come back?"

"Soon, I hope. Keep my skis waxed."

Now his laugh was hearty. He knew as well as she that waxes must be chosen for snow conditions and temperature. No waxless skis for them.

"Be sure to telephone," he said before they disconnected. "I'm a father. I worry always."

Which made it all the more remarkable that he'd never objected in the least way to her decision to join the Jegertroppen.

She was still sitting on the edge of the bed naked when she looked around and saw Trace with a towel wrapped around his narrow hips. He had leaned his shoulder against the doorjamb and folded his arms. Only then did she realize that she'd been speaking in Norwegian. "My father," she explained.

"Is he all right?"

"He was wondering about me and when I'd come back. He said he's in a desk job now but the mountains keep him young." She tilted her head, staring at Trace, yearning, and then her mind produced one of its irritating flips.

"Trace? If we need to tell someone about this, it should be my father."

Trace straightened. "You're probably right. He'd be the last person in the world to want to put you in danger."

"I'm sure of it. And he knows a great many people. He would know who to trust."

Hillary looked almost sadly at Trace. The moment was gone. Standing, she reached for the last clean clothes she had. He had already headed to his own bedroom.

But she had only a limited amount of time to find out what had happened to Brigid and her husband.

Sometimes life wasn't nice.

MORNING ARRIVED WITH no more in the way of answers. Hillary moved laundry from the washer to the dryer. Without comment they'd begun to wash their clothes together. There weren't many.

"I would have done that," Trace said.

She closed the dryer door, turning it on, then faced Trace. "I know you would have. You can do the folding."

"Fair enough."

Exhaustion rode them both. Lack of sleep with a heavy dose of mental fatigue. Running around in circles wasn't very rewarding.

Hillary made her oatmeal and topped it with a coddled egg. Trace opted for some kind of hash full of fried potatoes. And coffee. Always coffee.

"One more stab at that photo," Trace said. "Later if you need to sleep first."

"I just want to finish this," she admitted. "Like you, I want answers. We don't have enough here to take to anyone. We may have an indirect answer to what happened, though. Is that enough for you?"

"Is it enough for you?"

Brigid appeared in her mind's eye, a laughing Brigid with a heart of gold. "No." Her answer was short.

"Me neither."

Hillary stirred her oatmeal, mixing it with the egg, then began eating. After a few minutes, she spoke. "Brigid wanted to join your Army Rangers. I think I mentioned that."

He nodded.

"Was she always trying to keep up with you and Allan?"

Trace appeared surprised. "I don't know why she would have wanted to. We were always trying to keep up with her. Anyway, she probably would have tried for the Rangers right off, except at the time they weren't accepting women."

"They are neglecting a good resource."

His answer was dry. "Funny how men often miss that. Maybe we should read more history. From Boadicea to Joan of Arc. And then all the Celtic women who terrified the Romans by riding naked into battle. Lots more, I'm convinced."

"Camp followers, as you call them, often fought alongside their men. What a disparaging name."

"Well, it keeps them in their proper place, doesn't it?"

One corner of her mouth lifted. "What is my proper place?"

"Valkyrie," he answered promptly. "I give you your due."

She didn't doubt it.

After a quick cleanup, both felt refreshed, so they went back to the office.

"I don't know how far we'll get before we crash," Trace remarked.

"Farther than we are. I'm too awake now."

They returned to the photograph, convinced that if there was any answer, it had to be there.

Hillary offered a suggestion. "Let's look closely at the shadow that Brigid is making instead of the entire photo. There may be a reason her shadow crosses the shadow of the sign."

"Like her rifle crosses her," Trace agreed, sounding rather interested. He printed out two photo-quality prints and handed her one. "Allan must have had a magnifying glass somewhere."

Hillary studied the picture as Trace hunted through drawers. "I'm going to need spectacles after this."

"I'll join you."

"What makes you think Allan might have had a magnifying glass? Few young people do."

He glanced over his shoulder. "Because he probably spent almost as much time as we have looking at that picture." He sat up holding a rectangular glass. "Found it. Now I think I'll print out all the color reductions we did, to see the differences side by side."

"Good idea."

There were three desk lamps, surprising given that only two people had ever worked here, but for the first time they turned them all on and twisted them until they illuminated the photos brightly.

He asked, "You want to use the magnifier first?"

She accepted it and bent forward, wondering if her back would ever be straight again.

FROM EACH COPY, Trace had already screened out colors, starting with one color at a time, then moving on to screening out colors that didn't noticeably affect the photo.

One of the articles had said that doing so might reveal an image within the image. So far no go. But ever one to press on against ridiculous odds, he had then pixelated the photo, dividing it into tiny squares.

But Hillary was right about the angle of the shadows. It wouldn't be beyond Brigid to have considered such a thing, aligning it as closely as she possibly could with her rifle. And crossing the shadows. There wasn't a doubt in Trace's mind that Brigid had sent a message. Or that Allan might have found it, given how he had labeled the photo.

Just as he was about to fade from fatigue, Hillary gave his heart a jump start.

"Trace, look at these pixels. I can almost make out a word. Am I imagining it?"

No, she wasn't.

EVERY HUMAN NEEDED REST. It was the reason sentries fell asleep on duty. It was the reason people crashed cars because they were having microsleeps as their brains tried to rest.

Hillary and Trace reached that point a couple of hours later. They had what looked like it might be a name, whether first or last, they couldn't tell. Clearly Brigid had linked it to the sign behind her. They needed more.

But when a person starts hallucinating when awake, the mind is screaming a message. Eventually they had no choice but to tumble into bed.

They wound up in Hillary's bed, spooned but too tired to take advantage of the moment. Too busy trying to think about what they had found. Sleep, however, was a merciless taskmaster and took them away before they could solve anything or enjoy anything.

It all would have to wait. Outside, snow began to fall again, wrapping the world in the cold silence of a grave.

STAN WITHERSPOON WAS jangling too much to sleep. His eyes felt gritty; his head ached, feeling ten times larger than it was. His hands wouldn't stop trembling.

All this for money?

He despised himself and considered suicide, then backed away. He was afraid of dying, or he wouldn't be in this mess.

He should have just walked off the job in Afghanistan. Just quit. Instead he'd been so full of himself he'd bragged about how he'd taken care of Brigid Mannerly.

At first the boss had been pleased. Stan needed that

approval. But then everything had changed. The cage had been rattled.

Which brought him here, to a long road to nowhere. He wondered if he could successfully change his identity, then doubted it. He couldn't change his fingerprints, for one thing. Then there was the bigger problem: he had no idea how to get the necessary papers. He didn't know anyone or of anyone.

So there was just Stan on a dark Wyoming night while snow fell. It was probably his funeral shroud, he thought bitterly.

Then a germ of an idea was born. Just a germ. He tried to wrangle it into something he could use, but his mind was too far gone. He popped some pills for his headache, then lay down.

He damn well needed some sleep or he was going to lose it.

WHEN TRACE AND HILLARY AWOKE, thin gray light peeped through a small crack in the curtains. It wasn't going to be a beautiful day by the looks of it.

They lay face to face, their drowsy eyes meeting.

Trace spoke, his voice rough from sleep. "You know what I'd like to do with you? But we're hot on the trail now and you've got to go home soon. And don't argue with me. Your father is already phoning."

Hillary would have loved an excuse but knew he was right. Her father was growing concerned or he never would have called. He'd been giving her freedom to live her life as she saw fit ever since she'd approached adulthood. He'd never watched over her every moment.

There'd be time to love each other again when they'd come to the bottom of this. Time if she had to wrest it from Freya herself.

Slowly she stretched then walked down the hall to the laundry room. Fresh clothes. A fresh day. A fresh search.

God, Brigid, what did you get us into?

Except Brigid hadn't meant to get them into anything. She'd wanted Allan to know what was going on. She probably never thought it would cost her life. She'd probably imagined that Allan could get to the bottom of it from a safe distance.

No distance was safe.

AFTER A BREAKFAST of oatmeal for Hillary, scrambled eggs with cheese for both of them and a stack of toast for Trace, they headed to the office. Each carried a mug of the endless coffee with them and resumed their close inspection of the photos.

"Okay," Trace said. "We've made out the name Stanley. It could be either a first or last name, which hardly gets us anywhere."

She nodded agreement. "Can you imagine calling Briggs and Holmes to ask if they have an employee with the first or last name of Stanley?"

"I don't need to imagine it. They'd either slam down the phone or laugh. Neither would be useful at all. Well, if Brigid went to all this trouble, there must be another name in here somewhere."

They moved on to a different part of the shadow, hopeful as they had not been before.

A while later, Trace shocked her out of her intense focus, an intensity that was working her steadily toward a headache.

"You're beautiful," he said.

She pivoted, surprised, to look at him.

"Non sequitur, I know. But every time I glance at you, I see you all over again."

She felt her face heat slightly with an unaccustomed blush.

"Tell me to get back to work, my Valkyrie."

She drew a sharp breath. *His* Valkyrie? Oddly, she didn't mind at all.

"Okay, I'm out of line." He shrugged, smiling ruefully. "Brigid wanted to be like you, not like Allan and me."

"How can you know that?"

"Because I see all that's admirable in you. I'm sure Brigid did, too. Anyway, I apologize. Way out of line."

After a moment, she answered, "I didn't think so."

"Thank God. I don't usually just blurt things."

"You can blurt pretty things to me anytime you want." Then, following a strong, unrestrained impulse, she leaned forward and kissed him lightly on the lips. "My warrior from the skies."

That drew a broad smile from him. "That's the nicest way I've ever heard that." Then he shook his head. "Two warriors need to get back to work. I know you're leaving soon, Hills. Can't be avoided. But I'm going to miss you like hell."

Then, out of the blue, he was back in Afghanistan, in the midst of a firefight with shots raining down from the ridges above. He'd never know what triggered it. It had gotten better over the months of rehab, but here it was again, at the worst time possible. Was there ever a good time?

HILLARY SAW THE thousand-yard stare replace the usual warmth in Trace's gray eyes, turning him icy, stiffening him. Then he jumped up, knocking over his chair, hurrying from the room.

She followed immediately. "Trace?"

"Leave me the hell alone. Just get out of the way!"

He didn't know where he was going, just somewhere in his attempt to escape the tsunami of memories that took over his mind, that transported him to other places, other horrors. Bleeding, the repeated vibration of a rifle firing in his hands. The deafening sound of launching RPGs, thunderous explosions. Blood and gore, bodies shredded.

It had escaped his control. He couldn't fight it now. It had won.

HILLARY HAD A pretty good idea of what was going on, but she knew there wasn't a thing she could do about it except try to prevent him from harming himself while he relived battles. Relived not being able to trust anyone, not even the Afghans who had patrolled with him.

She'd learned that the hard way. She had a bullet scar on her upper arm, a graze but still a lesson. Friendly faces could conceal enmity.

Interesting, she thought distractedly, that neither of them had asked about the other's scars except that once

when she asked about his face. It was as if they didn't
see them. As if they'd assumed and understood.

But as for Trace, he stumbled around the house then
broke out the back door, hurrying until he fell facedown
in the snow. In the posture of an infantryman holding
a gun forward to shoot.

If she touched him now, he might turn on her, might
perceive her as an enemy. She had to stand over him
and watch. God, she wanted to be able to do something
for him. Anything to yank him back.

He wasn't dressed for the snow or the cold. If he
didn't rise from this ice soon, he could grow hypother-
mic. Maybe even get frostbite.

Finally she did the only thing she could think of. In
her harshest, strongest *kaptein* voice she ordered him,
"Mullen! Soldier, stand up, damn it. On your feet *now*!"

At first he only stiffened more. Then as the order
penetrated, he rose to his feet cautiously, looking
around.

Keeping her voice stern, she said, "The firefight is
over, soldier. Get your butt back to the operating base."
Thank God she'd listened to enough American officers
to know the slang.

As he began to slip out of memories, his face slowly
changed, losing its hard edge. It wasn't over yet, but at
least he headed back into the house. She followed him,
but he stormed into his bedroom and slammed the door
in her face.

"Leave me!"

She didn't go away. Instead she stood guard, ready
for anything. If he burst out of there looking to create

mayhem, her hands would be enough. She clenched and unclenched her fists, preparing. Her heart ached for him.

These things took time, but she would have waited until the moon fell from the sky.

MORE THAN TWO HOURS passed before Trace emerged from his room. Without a word, Hillary motioned him to the kitchen and began to pump him full of hot chocolate. "Drink," she ordered.

Still appearing a bit dazed, he didn't argue.

She wondered if he'd eat oatmeal. He'd never shown any interest. He needed food. Food and sugar. She pawed through Maude's bounty and eventually came up with a couple of pieces of peach cobbler and heated them in the microwave.

She pushed the plate in front of him. "Eat."

At first he did so automatically, but gradually the present time returned. "You should have some of this."

"You need it more than I do. I'll find something else."

"Time for another trip to Maude's."

Relief flooded her. He was on the way back. All the way back.

Eventually he spoke again. "I'm sorry."

"For what? PTSD? We all have it to varying degrees. You just had a bad round."

He raised his gaze to her. "You too?"

"Believe it. I'm just lucky."

It was a while before he spoke again. Two more cups of hot chocolate. Then hot cider, as if the cold penetrated to his very bones.

"Did I hear you giving me orders?" he asked.

"Oh yes. You heard my best command voice. At least it brought you out of the snow."

He winced. "Like that, huh?"

"Oh well. You're in one piece. Mostly."

"I have no idea what triggers it."

"Who needs a reason? Maybe it's staring at that photo of Brigid. Maybe some sound I didn't notice. Or maybe nothing at all."

"Makes me sadly unpredictable. It's also embarrassing."

"I himmelens navn."

"What?"

She sighed. She'd spoken in Norwegian again. "Oh, for heaven's sake."

"Disgust, huh?" He appeared to brace himself for bad news.

"With your apology and embarrassment, yes. I was *worried* about you, especially when you were facedown in the snow. I was *not* disgusted."

"Thank God for that." A faint humor was beginning to reappear. "Something for you to eat?"

She returned to the refrigerator, pulling out a soggy-looking steak sandwich. "Share with me. My stomach aches right now."

"I'm sorry."

"Stop. I did that to myself. I could have just left you to it and gone back to the photo or found a book to read. You didn't *make* me feel anything." Except sorrow that he had to endure it.

"Pity. There are a lot of things I'd like to make you feel, and that's not one of them."

Relaxation began to return to her, and she smiled. "We'll try that later."

"Just don't skip town before we do."

"I could not imagine it." After a couple of mouthfuls of the steak sandwich—at least the meat was still good—she rose and opened the curtains over the sink. "Snowing."

"Maybe it'll never stop this year."

She laughed. "You're spoiled."

"Maybe so."

"My father is already speaking of putting on his skis. Of the two of us heading into the mountains to camp."

"In weather like this?"

"Of course. If we stayed in the house all winter, suicide might become a rising problem."

"Likely along with the endless nights."

She eyed him as she returned to eating. "You might like them."

He wiggled his eyebrows. "Especially the endless nights."

"You have a dirty mind."

"I'm proud of it, too."

After they cleaned up, they discussed what to do next.

"We need more food here," Trace said practically. "We've managed to eat through most of what Maude gave us. The diner or the grocery?"

She considered. "I am not happy to leave the house unprotected. Not after the theft of the letters."

"At this point, I don't care. We'll carry the photos with us in an envelope."

Thus it was decided. Hillary had to admit a walk

would be very welcome. Stretching her legs with a steady stride instead of a run. Feeling the cold on her cheeks, breathing icy air, watching snow fall. As close to home as she would get here.

They bundled up and walked with a fast stride, this time to the grocery, joking about how neither of them liked to cook.

"Is there anywhere I can get cross-country skis?" she asked.

"Rent them, you mean? I think so. We can stop on the way back from the grocery."

That made her feel even better. Maybe Trace would join her. The traditional form of cross-country skiing, unlike the new form that was more like speed skating, was more like walking. Many people mastered it quite quickly.

At the grocery, they focused on items they could eat cold and items that were easy to cook, which included some frozen entrées. The butcher, Ralph, called them over and asked Hillary if she'd like him to order more fish for her.

"Please," she said with a smile. "Salmon and cod, if you can get them."

"Frozen or fresh?"

"I'd prefer fresh but frozen salmon will do. I already have frozen cod."

Ralph grinned. "I'll yank my contact's leg on that salmon again."

She felt pretty good as they departed the grocery with filled plastic bags. Then at the sports store, she found her rentals. She even persuaded Trace to try.

The boots were an easy fit for her, but the store owner eyed Trace.

"Do you have any idea how few people of your size want them?" He sighed and pawed through the boxes stacked nearly to the ceiling. "Hey," he said happily. "Size twelve. Now what about gaiters and socks and poles?"

They left fully equipped along with large backpacks that would carry almost everything they had bought at the grocery and the sporting goods store. The skis and poles they carried over their shoulders. Waxless skis, but beggars couldn't be choosers.

"Success," Trace said as they strode home.

"I think so. Now we have to decide when."

"Since the roads are a mess and we can't run, let's make it soon."

But when they reached the house, an envelope waited on the front porch, taped to the door.

"I think skiing just went off the schedule," Trace said.

Hillary pulled the envelope off the door. "Be careful when we open it. There might be fingerprints."

"I thought of the same thing. But gloves."

She regarded the envelope unhappily. Gloves. In this weather they were already wearing them. "The letter inside."

Trace was already unlocking the door. "Maybe. God, I hope it's useful."

Chapter Fifteen

Inside, they scrambled to put away frozen items or food that needed to be refrigerated. The envelope lay on the table as if it mocked them, seeming to grow brighter with each passing minute.

At last, with all the foodstuffs put away, their skis and accoutrements propped in the hallway, they sat as one to regard the envelope.

"What's your guess?" Trace asked Hillary. "A threat or information?"

"A threat," Hillary decided. "Given what happened to Allan and possibly Brigid."

"My feeling exactly." Rising, he went to get a filleting knife from the butcher block, then pulled on his glove liners once again. "Me or you?"

"You," she answered. She ran her gloved fingers over it. "Too thin to be threatening."

"Unless it contains powdered anthrax." A horrifying possibility.

"This man could have used that on Allan. He prefers blunter methods."

"I'd be inclined to agree, but we don't know that we're dealing with the same man."

When he said that, she reached out for the envelope. "Let me."

"Like hell."

She looked at him and realized he wasn't going to give ground on this. He'd already had a bruising day for his ego, and he was past caring that she was a soldier as well. She leaned back.

With the filleting knife in hand, he slipped it under a corner of the envelope and sliced carefully, a straight line across the top.

"Hold your breath," Trace said.

She knew an order when she heard one, and she obeyed, but only after saying, "Hold yours as well."

He cocked an eye at her. "You think I'm stupid?"

"Never, but if you're going to warn me, you should be warned, too."

His grin didn't quite make it. A good attempt, though. "What's sauce for the goose is sauce for the gander, right?"

She smiled back, although she didn't feel like smiling at all.

She watched intently as Trace slid a piece of paper out of the envelope. It sported a variety of colors. No powder showed or lifted into the air.

"Oh hell," he said, looking at the sheet. "Have we slipped into bad movie?"

"This is real."

"When did the movies ever care about that? No powder that I can detect. You?"

Impatient, Hillary rose and came around the table. Crooked cutout letters covered the page.

If you want to know what happened to Mannerly, meet me alone. More to come.

"Aw hell," Trace said. "Taunting."

"Basically useless, too. How long will he make us wait?"

"Until he tires of his game."

The hours ahead stretched until they looked like days.

THE GAUNTLET HAD been thrown, Hillary thought. A challenge.

"We've got to prepare anyway, Hills. I don't think he plans a meeting in the middle of town."

"Not likely." She pursed her lips. "Okay, he probably doesn't have our kind of experience and training."

"I doubt it," he agreed.

"The skis may be more useful than I thought. I can see it, Trace. You just have to accept it."

As if he followed her thoughts, he said, "Okay. He probably wants to meet *me*. You'll have to put your skills to the test. Ski ahead of the time of the meeting and find a good, concealed location."

"Exactly what I was thinking."

Trace's mouth twisted. "I don't believe he's going to be ready for an armed Valkyrie. I can just imagine you showing him your kind of hell."

"We need a weapon or two."

"Obviously I can't carry one. I'll look in Allan's gun

locker. I'd be surprised if he doesn't have an AR-15 or AK-47. Semiauto. You want me to alter one to full auto?"

Hillary shook her head. "If I have a decent scope, I won't need more than one shot."

"Try not to kill him," Trace said dryly. "We need the information."

She answered just as dryly, "I learned a lot about shooting around body armor. Center mass won't do it. Nor will hitting an artery or his head."

"We understand each other."

THE WAITING HAD BEGUN. Trace was the first to admit that he wasn't good at waiting. He wanted action.

Hillary didn't seem any happier about it, but when she asked him to pull out the photos, he took them out of the plastic bag that had been tucked under his jacket.

"Might as well," he said.

An hour later, her phone rang again. He gathered it was her father, who must be unusually worried, to judge what she'd said about his previous call. He listened to Norwegian flow from her lips and decided it was a pretty language. He wondered if he'd ever be able to learn any of it.

When she disconnected, he said, "Your father?"

"Yes."

"I thought he didn't hover."

"Hover?" It took her a minute to understand, then she grinned. "Not usually. This time he's even more concerned because he can't imagine any good reason why

I would be taking a holiday here. He must have looked up Conard City on a map."

"That would certainly raise questions. We're not on a list of anyone's preferred vacation destinations. At least we have mountains. What did you tell him?"

"That I'm on a mission. Then I thanked him for his concern and told him that I thought a squad of Norwegian special ops here would mess things up."

Trace laughed outright. "It certainly would. Sounds like a father to me."

She shrugged. "Just trying to be helpful. But this is hardly enemy territory."

Trace's expression changed. "I have no doubt that the two of us can handle this guy." He paused. "Before we get back into the photos again, I think I need to check the gun safe and give you a chance to adjust the scope."

They found a good selection of rifles, mainly for hunting. There was indeed an AR-15, semiautomatic. Legal in this gun-loving state and country.

From inside the mudroom with the door open so that no one could see, Hillary sighted through the scope. "I need to fire a few shots to be sure."

"There's a gun range just outside town. I doubt it's busy today. Wanna go?"

She nodded. This had to be done exactly right. Together they disassembled the rifle and cleaned it with the gun oil from the locker. Then they loaded it, still broken down, into a backpack so it wouldn't be identifiable. Trace added some high-powered binoculars when he picked up a box of shells.

THE GUN RANGE owner waved them in. "No charge today. All my customers are out hunting and aren't interested in practicing right now. Have at it."

"Let's wait," Trace said to Hillary. "Make sure we weren't followed. By the way, I hate waiting, in case I haven't said so."

"I as well. I didn't see anyone around on the way out here."

"Me neither, but extra caution never hurts."

They waited over twenty minutes while Trace scanned the surrounding area for any movement. Then Hillary quickly reassembled the AR-15 and loaded it with the bullets Trace handed her.

The clip could hold ten rounds. She took each shot at the target cautiously, adjusting the scope several times before she hit dead center three times in a row.

She locked the scope in place, and they once again disassembled the rifle. On the way back, they kept a sharp eye out for anyone who might be watching.

The road was deserted until they reached the edge of town. Even then the streets didn't appear busy.

"I think we made it," Trace remarked.

"I'm not too worried about it. He'll want you to come alone and probably unarmed. He won't be expecting me."

THE NEXT NOTE arrived overnight, left silently on the door. This one was also a mash of cutout letters, and the message was straightforward.

Six p.m. at old mining town. Mullen alone and unarmed.

Hillary looked at Trace. "You know where that is?"

"It's a landmark. Easy to get to, familiar to everyone, but it'll be deserted at this time of year." He looked at her. "Hills, it'll be deep twilight by then. Sunset is around six thirty. You know what the mountains do."

"I know. But it won't be dark enough to stop me." She glanced at the clock. "I should leave here soon to give me time to set up and get there without being noticed."

He sighed. "I don't like this. There are a whole lot of ramshackle and run-down buildings for him to hide in."

She shook her head. "I know what to do if he does. I'll be fast even on those no-wax skis, and skis are very quiet. I've done it before. Just give me directions."

That proved easy enough to do. The mining town was marked on the local map, and Allan had one folded on his desk, now buried in papers.

"There's no signal out there except on satellite phones. You won't have GPS."

"The map is all I need."

Of course it was, Trace thought. Of course. He went to find her a compass.

Chapter Sixteen

Hillary slipped away just after noon. She headed out the front in plain sight, and he watched her cart her skis and poles over her shoulder. Everything else was in a heavy backpack, her ski shoes and gaiters covering any outline of the rifle parts.

She walked away toward the east end of town, the opposite direction from the mining town. He saw her stop several people, and, whatever she said, they pointed east. Maybe asking them if there was a level place where she could use her skis.

Misdirection.

She strolled as if she had all the time in the world.

Then she disappeared from his sight. He could only guess where she'd gone to begin her westward trek.

Once again he had to wait. Only this time he worried as well. He eyed her cell phone left on the table so that if her father called again there would be no accidental ring in her pocket. Then he called the sheriff, Gage Dalton, and asked if there was any surreptitious way to get him a satellite phone and some zip cuffs. He didn't explain why, and Gage didn't ask. He just said, "Let me know."

Trace could do no more now except imagine the worst.

What he couldn't face was the possibility that something might happen to Hillary. As upset as he'd been about Allan, he wasn't sure he could survive her loss.

HILLARY ENJOYED HERSELF. Misdirection was part of her training while keeping watch for a route where she could safely change her course. It felt great to be on a mission again.

She found her place, then headed south. She didn't want anyone to see her ski away to the west. This walk was longer, but houses and people thinned out until there was nothing. She kept going for another two kilometers, then stopped to put on her skis.

If anyone was watching now, it would all look normal. Perhaps the land to the east that people had pointed out would provide a less challenging snow cover. This area had brush sticking up through the snow.

Well, she'd dealt with that before.

Skis on and locked, poles in hand, she began moving steadily west. Familiar. So familiar to her from training, from missions, from childhood. Her body fell into comfortable rhythms, and the faint sound as she swooshed through the snow reminded her of better times.

So far it was wonderful.

The slope began to rise, also familiar. When she reached a thick stand of evergreens, she pulled out the folded map and the small compass from her pocket.

Experience told her she'd reach the mining town shortly after four. Soon enough to check the lay of the land and choose her ground.

In the meantime, she had nothing to think about except the pleasure of her movements.

And about Trace. He was like a jack-in-the-box in her head, popping up again and again. The face she had come to love. The voice that either soothed her or drove her to the brink of desire.

If anything happened to him, she doubted she would be happy ever again.

SHORTLY AFTER FIVE, Trace left the house, headed for the mining camp and thanked God he had four-wheel drive with studded tires on his SUV. Renting it instead of a car had been expensive, but given the time of year, he hadn't wanted to screw around worrying about money.

The roads were terrible after the fresh snow. Beneath that layer was ice, gripped by the studs. If it got too bad, he had tire chains.

Trace had been up to the mining town many times in his youth. Dangerous as it was, pocked by collapsing mines, teens still went there. A favorite hangout away from adults unless one of the deputies or game wardens happened on them. All the warning signs got ignored. A chain-link fence meant to protect people had been cut so many times that the county had given up. It lay rusted and flat in places, an unheeded alert.

As the snow deepened, nobody would expect teens to be there.

It was a great choice for an isolated meeting. It would

give the guy a chance to watch him. Trace never believed the man would arrive unarmed. No, the perp intended to get rid of a problem. As he had with Allan. As he may have done with Brigid.

Anger simmered in Trace's veins, but it was an anger that cleared his head. Heightened his senses.

He'd been in situations like this before. They didn't scare him.

HILLARY SIGHTED THE mining camp at quarter after four. Plenty of time. She chose her position with the broadest view of the deteriorating town and the best concealment. Looking through her scope she surveyed the sinkholes, judging her skis would carry her safely over most of those pits. She memorized those she needed to be wary of.

Then she assembled the rifle and loaded it. Ready except for one thing.

She gathered snow-covered deadfall. She dug a body-size pit six inches deep. Then she crawled beneath the branches and waited. If the man came this way and happened to find her, he'd meet her rifle before he finished pulling away her cover.

The continuing snow protected her as well. She was prepared.

STAN WITHERSPOON SUFFERED anxiety as he waited at the mining village. He saw the SUV park about a hundred yards back in some wheel ruts that made it appear that damn vehicle might never get out. Good. He wanted Mullen stuck.

And he was glad to see Mullen alone. Nothing else around here had stirred in the last hour or so.

He surveyed the area and still saw no one and nothing as Mullen walked to the town and began pacing back and forth in front of the village. He'd come alone. The only question was if he was armed. Stan's mind leaped away from that possibility. He had to deal with it.

Stan was armed. He pulled a pistol out of his pocket and removed the safety catch. Only then did he hold it in front of him and approach Mullen. "Hands up!"

Mullen complied.

At this point Stan began to feel smart. He couldn't take Mullen and the woman out at the same time. That would have made him stupid.

But any way he looked at it, Mullen was the bigger threat given his background. Once Mullen was gone, the woman might just leave town. Or, if she knew anything and stayed, well, she was just a soldier. Stan was a soldier, too. Or had been.

One of the things Stan had learned in training was not to approach closely with a gun. Especially with a man like Mullen. He stood back at a safe distance.

"Do you want to know what happened to Allan? Why he had to die? Why Brigid had to die?"

"That's what I'm here for."

Stan was relieved Mullen made no move at all. One shot, maybe to his knee, whatever, would be enough to put Mullen down until Stan could kill him.

But Stan needed to get things off his chest. It wouldn't satisfy him just to kill. He hated being a murderer. He had to explain himself so this guy would understand.

"Brigid caught me moving arms to the insurgents. She saw me doing it twice, and I didn't think she was stupid."

"She certainly wasn't," Mullen answered.

Stan wanted to shrug, but his conscience was rearing up again, and he needed to get it all out. To explain how he had come to this. "I gave the insurgents an RPG and told them to take her out."

Trace drew a sharp breath. "Why, you…"

"Don't bother. I know what I am. I thought it was over. I have a boss, you know that?"

"I didn't until now."

Witherspoon heard the edge in Mullen's voice, saw the man clench his fists, even though they were up in the air. "Don't move or I'll shoot right now and you'll never know why I killed Allan Mannerly."

Mullen was silent for a few seconds but didn't move. "Go on." His voice was taut with threat, but Witherspoon didn't believe it.

Besides, he was going to die one way or another unless he got this cleaned up. Then he had a thought. "That woman isn't here somewhere, is she?" He started once again to scan the surrounding area but wasn't too worried. After an hour of observation, he was sure no one else was there. But he needed to ask anyway.

"She's a woman." Mullen's voice sounded scornful.

Just a woman. Mullen made a good point. Braver now, Witherspoon continued. "That Mannerly guy did something or said something. All I know is the cage started rattling, and I was caught in it. I didn't want to kill anyone!"

"I believe you," Mullen answered.

Stan didn't quite believe *him*, but it didn't matter. He needed to have his say, then he'd erase this part of the problem.

"My boss knew information had gotten out. He was uneasy. So he told me to get my butt over here, because he figured it was Brigid's husband who had warned someone else. I was sent to kill him any way I could."

Mullen growled but still didn't move.

"It was easy enough. The guy got drunk every night. I just told him I knew Brigid. He let me in. I don't think he ever noticed I was carrying my pistol." He paused. "Funny, but everyone around here has a gun, and some of them carry them in town. Nothing unusual."

Mullen gave a tight nod.

"So, when Mannerly got drunker, almost passed out, I finished it. Blew his brains out. Left the gun beside him. I thought I was done, but then you started yelling and my boss got even more worried."

Mullen never flinched.

"He was afraid you knew something. So now I have to take you out. I don't like it. I'm not a murderer, but he'll kill me if I don't get this done."

Trace's voice grew thin as fine steel. "You want me to feel sorry for you? You're the victim in all this?"

"You gotta understand. And it doesn't matter if you don't want to." He waved his gun toward a nearby building. "Now get in there."

"Why should I?"

Stan had never expected that response. He waved his gun again.

Then a movement caught his attention, and when he turned he saw the wrath of hell skiing swiftly toward him, a rifle pointed straight at him. It cracked like thunder.

He thought he felt sharp pain in his knee, but before he knew for sure, Mullen had jumped him and thrown him to the ground. His gun was still in his hand. He started to move it, wondering who to shoot first.

Then the woman was standing over him, her rifle pointing straight at his head, and said, "I wouldn't use that pistol if I were you."

Mullen had his hands around Stan's throat, but not too tightly for him to breathe. Just enough to scare him.

"Who's she?" Stan asked thinly. "I was watching before you got here. I never saw her come. You said she wasn't here."

"She's a Valkyrie, you jackass. Trust me, you'll have plenty of time in jail to look it up."

Mullen rolled Witherspoon over and used zip cuffs on his wrists.

Then Trace said, "I suppose we need to put a tourniquet on him."

"Regrettably," the woman replied.

"Gage gave me his sat phone," Mullen told them both. "I called just as I arrived here. Armed response is on the way." Then he began to tie something around Stan's thigh.

The pain in Witherspoon's knee pierced his shock, and he began to shriek. All he wanted now was an ambulance and a huge dose of morphine.

Chapter Seventeen

Hillary sat in the first-class cabin of an airplane on the way to Tromsø, north of the Arctic Circle. She was eagerly looking forward to seeing her father. She'd asked for and received an extension to her vacation. She suspected Pa had something to do with that. Maybe having him behind a desk could be useful.

She turned her head and looked at Trace in the seat beside her. He was already staring at her, and she felt a shiver of pleasure.

He spoke. "That Witherspoon guy sang like a bird."

She nodded. "Even sold out his chief."

"I think he figured that years in prison might be better than being shot some dark night by his boss."

"You may be right."

Silence fell between them. Hillary liked it when he took her hand, gave it a squeeze then just held it. He made her heart sing.

Her father had taken the story from her and assured her he would deal with it. She hadn't asked for details because she knew her father. By the time he was done, everyone involved in these arms sales was going to be exposed to criminal charges. Every single one.

Brigid and Allan would be avenged.

Trace spoke again. "Your father. Will he like me, do you think?" It was not the first time he had asked.

"I've said so."

She had no doubt. Her father would see in Trace a reflection of himself. More, he would think a special ops soldier was well suited to her.

But Trace would not be returning to the Army. One of the saddest things he'd said to her was, "I'll never jump again."

He'd decided a desk job would drive him nuts. "If I ever doubted it, all that work we did trying to catch this killer taught me. No desk for me."

Now he flew with her to Norway after putting in for his medical discharge.

And she had to hope that he would like her home, her country. He certainly hadn't bought a return ticket.

She squeezed his hand. "Don't be nervous."

"Who, me?"

She laughed lightly. "He's another soldier like you."

"Yeah? I've never had to face down a spec ops officer and tell him I want to marry his daughter."

Her heart stopped. "Trace?"

"You heard me. And you can handle it, so tell me if you want me to shut up."

"Never," she answered, squeezing his hand tightly. "Never." The song in her heart grew louder.

"I don't do crazy things like this." He grinned. "I love you, you know."

"You're giving me that idea."

"I'll give you more of an idea later."

MAGNUS KRISTIANSEN MET them at the gate, tall and straight, his hair only slightly darker than his daughter's. Hillary beelined straight for him, for his smiling face, pulling Trace along with her. Her father gave her a big bear hug then looked at Trace.

"This is him?" he asked in Norwegian.

She answered in English. "This is Trace Mullen, the man I love. We're going to be married."

Now it was Trace's turn to feel a song in his heart. Especially when he looked at Hillary's father and saw a big smile.

"Just promise to live in Norway," Kristiansen said.

Looking at Hillary, Trace answered, "I think I can promise that."

* * * * *

Don't miss other romances in Rachel Lee's thrilling Conard County: The Next Generation series:

Available now from Harlequin Books

 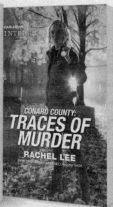

COMING NEXT MONTH FROM

⊕ HARLEQUIN

INTRIGUE

#2007 SAFEGUARDING THE SURROGATE
Mercy Ridge Lawmen • by Delores Fossen
Rancher Kara Holland's hot on the trail of a murderer who's been killing surrogates—like she was for her ill sister. But when Kara's trap goes terribly wrong, she's thrust headlong into the killer's crosshairs...along with her sister's widower, Deputy Daniel Logan.

#2008 THE TRAP
A Kyra and Jake Investigation • by Carol Ericson
When a new copycat killer strikes, Detective Jake McAllister and Kyra Chase race to find the mastermind behind LA's serial murders. Now, to protect the woman he loves, Jake must reveal a crucial secret about Kyra's past—the real reason The Player wants her dead.

#2009 PROFILING A KILLER
Behavioral Analysis Unit • by Nichole Severn
Special Agent Nicholas James knows serial killers. After all, he was practically raised by one and later became a Behavioral Analysis Unit specialist to enact justice. But Dr. Aubrey Flood's sister's murder is his highest-stakes case yet. Can Nicholas ensure Aubrey won't become the next victim?

#2010 UNCOVERING SMALL TOWN SECRETS
The Saving Kelby Creek Series • by Tyler Anne Snell
Detective Foster Lovett is determined to help his neighbor, Millie Dean, find her missing brother. But when Millie suddenly becomes a target, he finds himself facing the most dangerous case of his career...

#2011 K-9 HIDEOUT
A K-9 Alaska Novel • by Elizabeth Heiter
Police handler Tate Emory is thankful that Sabrina Jones saved his trusty K-9 companion, Sitka, but he didn't sign up for national media exposure. That exposure unveils his true identity to the dirty Boston cops he took down...and brings Sabrina's murderous stalker even closer to his target.

#2012 COLD CASE TRUE CRIME
An Unsolved Mystery Book • by Denise N. Wheatley
Samantha Vincent runs a true-crime blog, so when a friend asks her to investigate a murder, she's surprised to find the cops may want the case to go cold. Sam is confident she'll catch the killer when Detective Gregory Harris agrees to help her, but everything changes once she becomes a target...

YOU CAN FIND MORE INFORMATION ON UPCOMING HARLEQUIN TITLES, FREE EXCERPTS AND MORE AT HARLEQUIN.COM.

HICNM0621

SPECIAL EXCERPT FROM

⧫HARLEQUIN

INTRIGUE

*Police handler Tate Emory is thankful that
Sabrina Jones saved his trusty K-9 companion, Sitka,
but he didn't sign up for national media exposure.
Exposure that unveils his true identity to the dirty
Boston cops he took down…and brings Sabrina's
murderous stalker even closer to his target…*

*Read on for a sneak preview of
K-9 Hideout by Elizabeth Heiter.*

Desparre, Alaska, was so far off the grid, it wasn't even listed on most maps. But after two years of running and hiding, Sabrina Jones felt safe again.

She didn't know quite when it had happened, but slowly the ever-present anxiety in her chest had eased. The need to relentlessly scan her surroundings every morning when she woke, every time she left the house, had faded, too. She didn't remember exactly when the nightmares had stopped, but it had been over a month since she'd jerked upright in the middle of the night, sweating and certain someone was about to kill her like they'd killed Dylan.

Sabrina walked to the back of the tiny cabin she'd rented six months ago, one more hiding place in a series of endless, out-of-the-way spots. Except this one felt different.

HIEXP0621

Opening the sliding-glass door, she stepped outside onto the raised deck and immediately shivered. Even in July, Desparre rarely reached above seventy degrees. In the mornings, it was closer to fifty. But it didn't matter. Not when she could stand here and listen to the birds chirping in the distance and breathe in the crisp, fresh air so different from the exhaust-filled city air she'd inhaled most of her life.

The thick woods behind her cabin seemed to stretch forever, and the isolation had given her the kind of peace none of the other small towns she'd found over the years could match. No one lived within a mile of her in any direction. The unpaved driveway leading up to the cabin was long, the cabin itself well hidden in the woods unless you knew it was there. It was several miles from downtown, and she heard cars passing by periodically, but she rarely saw them.

Here, finally, it felt like she was really alone, no possibility of anyone watching her from a distance, plotting and planning.

Don't miss
K-9 Hideout *by Elizabeth Heiter,*
available July 2021 wherever
Harlequin Intrigue books and ebooks are sold.

Harlequin.com

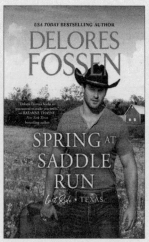